FIND YOURSELF

FIND YOURSELF

S. BREAKER

Zeta Indie Publishing

For my alternate self

Contents

I

Normal

***

"Laney…"

"Laney, I knew it was you."

"Laney, wake up."

"Wake up, sleepyhead."

Laney rolled over in her bed, groaning. "Five more minutes, Mom."

She heard her boyfriend, Kevin, chuckle under his breath.

Laney opened one eye to peek up at him but otherwise didn't move from under her covers. "Kevin, what are you doing here? Where's Stephanie?" She gave her dorm room a quick glance over.

Laney's room at her New England boarding school fit two single beds and two desks, but it looked even smaller at the moment. There was barely any space to walk on the floor, with the questionably-clean clothing, disarrayed stacks of books, and crumpled up pieces of paper, most of them Post-it notes, all strewn about. A stuffed rabbit that looked like it had seen better days was tucked underneath the bed across the way—her roommate, Stephanie's. The bed was empty, but still unmade, with its bed sheets having been dragged down almost to the floor.

Kevin was standing by the doorway with an amused grin on his face. "Time?" he prompted her.

She grimaced back at him, squinting in the bright light pouring in from the windows, before turning to the digital clock on her desk to check, and her eyes popped open.

8:45 a.m.

"Oh my god!" Laney jumped out of bed. "I overslept again!"

She hopped around the room in a frantic attempt to get ready, stubbing her toe on the corner of the desk leg, and yelping even more loudly as her heel landed hard on top of an electric cable under a sweater on the floor, before she made it to the little sink to brush her teeth, somehow managing to get dressed and ready.

She found Kevin back out in the hallway, leaning against the wall by the door. He whistled in amusement. "I think you just set a new record. It took you over five minutes yesterday."

Laney gave him a suffering look. "You know what, I think Janet likes you a little bit too much for an R.A. if she keeps letting you sneak into the girls' dorm like this."

"What can I say? You're a lucky girl." Kevin kissed her

forehead lightly before he gave her a once-over look, his forehead creasing in concern at the bags under her eyes. "Still having those weird dreams?"

Laney shifted uncomfortably as the two of them began walking down the hall.

To call her dreams in the last few months "weird" was a complete understatement. Obviously, dreaming was a normal thing for a person to do, despite how really vivid or how really strange they were. The only difference was that starting a few months ago, each of Laney's dreams would always devolve into the exact same one.

The dream that had only started out in fragments of images, buried by other dreams and memories, until it had started to surface more and more, getting even more disturbing as each replay invaded her subconscious every night.

The dream.

More like 'nightmare.'

The people in the dream have no faces, but what she always remembered clearly was—the pain. It would be everywhere, all at once—down her throat, through her chest, in her stomach, down her legs to her toes, all through her arms to her fingertips, inside her head, stinging her teeth, burning behind her eyeballs...

It always happened in the middle of the night and she would wake up in a cold sweat.

Confused. Bewildered. Panicked.

Suffice it to say, Laney hadn't been getting much sleep of late—*again.*

"What about meditation before going to sleep? Did you try those earplugs again? To block out the ambient noise?

What else can we try?" Kevin asked, for what seemed like the millionth time.

She rolled her eyes, having heard all this before. Then she shook her head. "I can't believe this. Darla is probably going to have to drag me to the nurse's office again. And here I thought I might actually manage to finish the year without having yet another health scare."

"We did figure it was just stress-related last time, right? Maybe you should take a break and go home again," Kevin suggested as he opened the door leading outside for her.

"I was just there for Thanksgiving," Laney told him, wrinkling her nose. "Besides, it's been...a bit weird at home. Well," she amended. "Really, it's been weird ever since the divorce. And now that Dad is seeing Gina, and Mom and Hank are still on the fourth trimester—let's just say I feel like there's just suddenly way too many people in my house."

"Oh what, that new baby not so much the bundle of joy they thought he would be?" he prompted as they hurried down the path heading toward the classrooms.

Laney chuckled. "So much fun! The house has been turned upside-down. I mean, I love the little guy—but man, can he crap!"

Kevin laughed. "Well, what did your parents say, about you not getting much sleep lately?"

"Nah, I didn't want to worry them," she said. "It probably *is* just stress. I mean, everything *is* coming down to the wire now with the last few weeks of school, not to mention college applications..." she trailed off, sounding overwhelmed.

Kevin grinned as he slung his arm around her shoulders. "You know what Dean Rosenthal says, high school graduation is a rite of passage, the end of easy, the end of life as we know it."

At those words, a shadow crossed Laney's face, but she shook off the unsettled feeling as Kevin went on.

"I mean, imagine it," he added cheerfully. "Next year, we'll be in college! It's an exciting time!"

Laney's expression was still somber. "Well, I know one thing's for sure." She stopped as they arrived at the door to her class. "I'll never make it through hell week and Professor Tanner's final without a decent night's sleep, so whatever is wrong with me, I better snap out of it, and fast," she told him.

Kevin gave her an encouraging soldier-on smile. "I'll pack you some Gatorade."

"Thanks, Kev. You're the best." She was leaning up to kiss him when the bell rang, and they both looked up. "Oh. Great." She frowned.

"Well, so much for your first class," Kevin smirked and gave her a quick peck on the cheek before scooting backward. "Now I have to get to class, too. See you later?" he prompted her, amidst the throng of students streaming past, coming out of the door.

"Yeah." Laney nodded, giving him a small wave as she watched him walk down the hall and disappear around the corner.

Fortunately, Laney had a free period next, and she only had to meet up with her best friend, Darla, so she didn't need to rush anywhere.

It only took about a minute before every student had relocated to their next classrooms, with doors shutting loudly, and then the hallway was empty again.

Laney looked around. The silence in the hallway seemed ominous, even with the bright fluorescent lights on the ceiling bouncing off the green linoleum floors.

Then again, everything to her lately felt ominous. No doubt caused by her freaky weird dreams. So much so that no matter how hard she tried to shake it, the feeling of unease stayed with her all day. And these dreams, they weighed on her. As though they were a warning. Of something impending. Something not good.

She sighed, turning on her heel to head toward the library to meet Darla. They were supposed to do some last-minute cramming for their French finals together.

Laney froze as the hallway before her blurred and everything turned gray. And when she looked up again, she was in the middle of a busy city intersection, surrounded by tall skyscrapers with mirrored windows, the images of cars and other vehicles zooming past her so vivid—so close, she could smell the exhaust fumes.

She coughed, stepping back.

And she was back in the school hallway, with the green floor and bright fluorescent light.

Laney looked around, disoriented.

"Laney!" Darla called out.

Laney jumped, startled, before turning to look.

Darla was waiting for her at the end of the hall, her hands on her hips. She waved her over.

Laney blinked to get her bearings before she walked up to Darla.

Darla noticed her stunned expression and looked at her strangely. "What's going on?"

She cleared her throat. "Uh, nothing. I was just..." She shook her head slowly. The truth was that Laney would have been more bewildered if that was the first time that it had happened. But it wasn't. It had been happening on and off for weeks. Except previously, she had dismissed the "hallucinations" as daydreams, as being simply her imagination going on overdrive.

But that day, it felt different. The hairs on the back of her neck were still standing up with an unidentified dread of something. The crosswalk had been so intensely real that she could still smell the fossil fuels burning her nose.

Laney met Darla's gaze.

Darla was still peering up at her with curious pale green eyes. "Let me guess, rough night? Again?"

She gave her a look and a short nod, as she was willing to admit to at least that, and she wasn't going to give her friend any more cause for concern if she could help it.

Darla patted her back in sympathy, but her tone was playful. "Why can't you be normal and dream about Hollywood hunks like the rest of us?"

Laney chuckled, her mood lightening.

"Well, come on then," Darla coaxed, leading the way to the library. "Those verbs aren't going to conjugate themselves, and some of us need at least a B to make up for last semester."

Laney made a face. "You mean a B+," she corrected. "I'm never forgiving you for making me take this class. Languages are so not my thing."

Darla turned back slightly to give her a meaningful shrug. "Who cares about languages when the teacher is so hot?"

Laney laughed to herself. "Fine, I'll admit Monsieur

Martin's accent is super hot, but he's like twenty-eight or something," she pointed out. "Besides," she dismissed with a wave. "Even my career counselor, Mrs. Pat, says I'm not likely to pursue French studies in college."

Darla raised her eyebrows. "Sounds like you've finally made a decision."

"Well, no," Laney replied. "It's just..." She pursed her lips. "You're lucky you already know what you want to be when you grow up."

"Hey, it's not me." Darla shook her head. "It's genetics. My dad's a composer. My grandfather was that guy that waves a stick at chamber orchestras—"

"A conductor?" Laney supplied with a smirk.

"Yeah, that, whatever," she said, waving her hand again. "My point is I've been bitten by the music bug." She paused. "You really not feeling the 'law' thing like your folks?"

Laney bit her lip in mockery. "Yeah, somehow I'm not super excited at the thought of all the mountains of paper-work, or arguing loopholes around legal precedents—"

"Sure, 'cause you just hate to argue," Darla remarked, a wry look on her face. "Don't you, Miss Moral Compass?"

Laney shot her a look. "Whatever." She shrugged. "I'm still in limbo. I feel like I'll forever be in limbo. And I have a sneaking suspicion that my actual expertise lies in absolutely nothing."

"Oh, cheer up, Laney," Darla chided as they arrived at the library. "Think about it, if we both manage to fail the French final, don't go to college, and get no job, then maybe that's exactly what the two of us will end up doing. Nothing."

Laney laughed. "Well, here goes 'nothing' then."

***

Applause.

The bell rang.

Laney blinked, snapping to alert.

"*Au revoir, Mademoiselle Carter.*" Monsieur Martin gave her a little wave as the rest of the class began to file out the door.

Darla was grinning from ear to ear as she escorted Laney out the door, her arms around her shoulders pompously. "That's right, people! My best friend," she announced as they exited the room.

Kevin met the two of them outside the classroom door. "Hey, guys. Ready for lunch?" He tilted his head, his forehead creasing as he noticed several people passing by patting Laney's back in congratulations. "What's going on?"

"Miss Thing here, suddenly the fluent French speaker," Darla said, pulling away to thump on Laney's back. "She totally aced the oral final!"

"What? That's great!" Kevin remarked, sounding surprised, but he also looked proud as he put his arm around her and they all walked toward the cafeteria. "You were so nervous about it. I'm so happy for you."

Darla turned to her, beaming. "Did you actually buy those language CDs like Monsieur Martin suggested? That was just absolutely amazing! And here I thought we both needed that cramming session this morning. Turns out I'm the only *perdante* here."

"Hey, guys," Laney started. "I think I need to take a nap."

She broke away from Kevin's grasp to step backward, looking uncomfortable.

"What's the matter, Laney?" Kevin gave her a concerned look.

"Nothing. I'm—I'm just really tired right now," Laney replied and turned to Darla again. "Hey, can you also tell Mr. O'Connor and Mrs. Hatchet that I'm not feeling well?"

Darla looked her over. "Sure, but *are* you not feeling well?"

"I'm fine," Laney insisted. "I think I just need to rest. I don't think I'm going to make the rest of my classes today."

"Maybe I should take you to the nurse's office—"

Laney blew out a breath, exasperated. "Jeez, Darla! Would you just—I'll be fine, I promise. Look, I just...need to get some shut-eye right now. Seriously." She gave them both re-assuring nods.

Kevin and Darla exchanged worried glances, but then Kevin just met Laney's gaze again. "Okay," he conceded. "But I'm checking up on you right after lunch."

"Me too," Darla chimed in with a nod.

"Fine. Great." Laney nodded quickly, walking backward away from them. But as she started to turn to leave, she stopped short and looked back at her friends. "Hey, thanks...guys."

Kevin gave her a good-natured grin. "See you later, Laney."

Darla mocked a salute at her. "*Au revoir.*"

Laney walked into the dorm and headed straight up the stairs. All she wanted was to lie down in her bed.

Things were starting to get out of hand. First, her getting up late again because of those hellish nightmares, then the intersection in the middle of the school hallway, then the French class…

Today, she thought. *There's something wrong with today.* Something majorly wrong.

She turned the corner and walked past a few doors to arrive at her room. But when she turned the knob on the door and swung it open, she gasped startled, as there was no longer a room there.

It wasn't that the room was darkened, even though in the middle of the afternoon, the yellow sun should have been streaming through her windows and onto her bed. No. The doorway just gaped upon a pitch-black emptiness.

No light. No sound. A void. A nothingness.

"What the—?" She took a half-step back so she wouldn't lose her balance and fall into the nothing.

Laney shut the door quickly, her hand still on the knob. *What is going on?* She looked around suspiciously, but it was the middle of a class day so the dorm hallways were empty.

She took a deep breath to collect herself, and after a moment, she gingerly turned the knob to open the door again and was absolutely relieved to see the inside of her room—as she'd expected.

The room was still a mess, much like it usually was during finals. But her roommate Stephanie was sitting on her bed.

She looked up when Laney opened the door. "Hey Laney," she greeted. "How did your French final go?"

Laney stared at her, still a bit mystified. "Uh…fine, it was fine. Hey," she started. "Did you…? Did I just open the door just now? I mean, before I did just now. Did I open the door twice? Did you see me?"

Stephanie shot her a weird look. "What?"

"You were in the room though, right? You've been in the room the whole time?"

"Yeah, since third period," she said. "I'm working on my History paper. I told you about that yesterday, remember?"

"Right," Laney mumbled. She blinked a few times again as though to clear her head.

She could have sworn there was definitely no room there when she had opened the door before, but if Stephanie had been in there since third period, exactly what door had she opened the first time?

Another shiver of dread ran up Laney's spine and she whirled around to rush off.

"Hey Laney, are you okay?" Stephanie called out after her.

"I'm fine!" Laney replied out loud, even as she clattered down the stairs, heading back out the dorm. Her pulse had begun to race in anxiety. She definitely had to find Kevin and Darla again. Whatever the hell was happening to her, it was getting worse, and there was no point hiding it anymore. She needed to tell someone. She needed help.

Laney crossed the quad lawn headed for the cafeteria. There were a few students picnicking in the garden as it was a nice, sunny day—one of the last ones probably this side of winter.

She passed two girls from her French class and when they both waved at her, with expressions of awe on their faces, Laney just managed a tight smile back as she walked faster.

Then she happened to glance up to see Jake Donovan from across the way.

Jake was a popular campus figure, captain of the hockey

team, quite a guy with the females from what she had heard, but they'd hardly ever crossed paths. They'd never had to. She didn't even think he knew her name.

He was standing near the pathway where the trees that lined the garden merged with the bushes. But he looked different today somehow.

She thought she caught him staring at her, but when she blinked to look again, he was gone.

2

Go Again

He appeared right before her, blocking her path.

Laney's eyes widened in fright, and she instinctively tried to run away, but he grabbed her from behind, his hand over her mouth so she couldn't scream.

"Sshhh," he shushed, even as she struggled against him as he pulled her back behind an empty pop-up booth for selling prom tickets. "Relax, Laney. It's me, it's me."

She tried to struggle more forcibly.

"Come on, you know me. Remember," he urged. "Please remember."

And Laney bit his hand.

He yelped out loud and sprang back, letting her go. "Why do you always do that?" he demanded, annoyed.

She whirled around. "Jake! What the hell do you think you're doing?" she demanded, yelling right to his face. "You can't just go sneaking up on people when they're alone like that!" She threw up her hands. "Why are you even talking to me anyway? Was that you I saw staring at me earlier? What is going on with you? What on earth are you wearing?" She made a face down at his strange clothes before looking back up at him. "And—what is up with your hair?"

Noah narrowed his eyes in frustration, impatience. Then without warning, he braced his hands on her shoulders. "Shut up, Laney," he ordered, his voice strained.

And before Laney knew what was going on, he had bent his head and caught her lips in his.

He kissed her deep, ardent—*familiar*—as though he knew her, as though he had known her all her life.

Noah's grip loosened when she stopped struggling and resigned herself to the intensity of his kiss. But she didn't kiss him back. He broke off slowly, his eyes still closed.

Laney's eyelids were heavy when she finally met his lustrous gaze. "Do I know you?" she whispered.

His voice almost faltered, "Yes."

But she didn't know him. She didn't remember.

Laney's eyes popped open and she pushed him away, hard. "My boyfriend Kevin is waiting for me," she relayed, pointedly.

Noah visibly clenched his jaw.

"I seriously don't know what the hell is going on with you, and what the hell you think this is, but maybe *you* also need a quick trip to the nurse's office," she suggested.

"Laney, I really need to talk to you," he said, an urgent look in his eyes.

"Look, Jake...that was um...very nice," she phrased carefully, starting to back away. "But I really have to go now. So if you want to alert your friends, who are no doubt all watching, that you've accomplished your little prank, then maybe we can all get to class," she said, before pausing. "Unless of course, you actually have some sort of rational explanation that you're maybe willing to share?" she prompted, an almost incredulous look on her face. She wasn't really sure why she wanted to give him the benefit of the doubt, but she did.

Noah shook his head, muttering, "I can't believe I have to go through all this with you again."

Laney shot him a stubborn look, even if she didn't fully understand. "Well, you're gonna."

He let out a sigh and paused for a moment. "Alright," he started. "My name is Noah—"

"But Jake—"

"He's not me, okay!" Noah threw up his hands at her interruption, quickly cutting her off. "*Yes*, we look alike, but we have different names, different personalities—*I* don't know why. That's just the way it is. Now, will you please, *for once*, let me finish before you say anything? I'm kind of on the clock here," he stated.

Laney looked taken aback at his seemingly extreme response, but she rolled her eyes and gestured for him to continue.

He sighed again, before calmly starting over. "My name is Noah. I'm from another parallel world. And about eight months ago, you helped me save my world *and* yours. Yes." He nodded, upon seeing her eyes widen again in response. "We have met before. And we've..." He hesitated. "Been through a lot together. I've saved your life many times and...you've saved mine."

Laney raised her hand as if to interject a question politely.

He stopped. "Yes?"

She smirked, whispering, "You're nuts."

He clenched his jaw again.

"If we have met before, then how come I can't remember?" she prompted.

"We gave you something to make you forget, so you could go back to your normal life," he replied.

Laney laughed. "That is absolutely impossible," she said. "And *even if* you were telling the truth, which is highly unlikely, if all of that did indeed happen eight whole months ago —that we'd already met and saved a bunch of parallel worlds together, then," she posited with a mocking tone. "What the hell are you doing back here?"

He met her gaze. "I'm here to save you again."

The gravity in the tone of his voice made Laney pause, that vaguely familiar chill running through her. She shook her head quickly to clear it. "Um, okay, I'm sufficiently freaked out now," she said. "So I think I'll just—" She gestured behind her, starting to walk away again. "Go."

"How long ago did the hallucinations start?" Noah called out with a casual tone.

Laney looked stunned. "What?"

He gave her a steady look. "Things not seeming to be where they should...suddenly finding yourself in different places altogether," he supplied. "Doing things you've never done before, things you didn't even know you could do."

She started to breathe heavily. "I spoke French fluently for fifteen minutes this morning." She looked up to meet his gaze, bewildered. "How do you...?"

He pursed his lips. "I'm sorry, Laney," he said, almost under his breath. "It's all my fault."

She was still frowning as she looked up at him, a sick feeling starting in her stomach.

Just hearing him describe what she'd been struggling through in the past few months only made the reality sink in even more. And the look on his face didn't make it seem like any of it was going to get any better. She swallowed hard, still trying to get a grip.

But after a moment, Noah raised his eyebrows at her in a somewhat impatient prompt. "Tick-tock, tick-tock." He tapped his wrist. "I've only got a limited-time anchor. I honestly didn't think it would take this long to come get you. I was obviously sorely mistaken."

Laney gave him a look of exasperated disbelief. "Well, excuse me while I grapple with every self-doubt that I've been fighting for the past few months. You have no idea what kind of hell I've been going through!"

A shadow crossed his face and his next words were gentler. "But do you believe me now?" He was holding her gaze intently, and Laney took a moment before nodding.

"Good," Noah said. "Because I need you to come with me."

Her gaze turned wary. "Where?"

Noah took her hand and led her through the thicket that lined the school walkway, emerging into a small clearing within the school backyard, out of view from anyone at the quad gardens.

Laney glanced around anxiously to check if anybody had noticed that she had disappeared through the bushes with *not*-Jake Donovan. But all the other students in the garden were busy with their lunches, talking and hanging out with their own friends, blissfully unaware of any life-altering phenomena going on.

She spotted Kevin and Darla among a small group of people across the garden. Darla was laughing. Someone tossed some Cheetos across the way. Kevin high-fived somebody.

Laney bit her lip, taking a slow deep breath before she turned back to Noah, who was then preoccupied with some type of gadget with a glowing holographic update display (HUD) hovering above his left forearm, tapping a few keys in mid-air.

Then he looked up.

Laney followed his gaze and she noticed a dense black ball seeming to form in mid-air. "What...the hell is that?"

The ball grew into a hole, getting bigger and bigger, its frayed edges spinning around its center. The wind rose up, whipping the leaves around them on the ground and Laney's hair around her face. Then she blinked, alarmed, as the sky seemed to instantly darken, but when she looked up, she could see that the afternoon sun was still in the sky, right where it was supposed to be.

And she realized that it wasn't so much that it was getting dark, but instead everything around her was changing in hue. She looked back up at Noah, puzzled. "Why is everything turning red?" she asked, over the increasing noise of the blowing gale.

"The quantum shear sucks in every spectrum of light—red goes last," Noah explained.

Laney's eyes were still wide as she stared at what was

tearing a hole right down the middle of her reality. "The quantum shear, you mean that swirling—"

"Yes, yes, swirling vortex of doom." He waved dismissively.

Her eyebrows snapped together. "Hey, you're not suggesting that we're actually going to go through that thing, are you?" she asked, taking a step back, looking horrified. "See, when you said you needed me to come with you, I'd assumed we were just going outside campus."

Noah gave her a look. "Believe me, you *have* done this before."

She let out a loud sigh. "Well, excuse me. To me, it feels like the first time."

He was entering the last of the quantum shear calibrations on his HUD, not looking at her.

"What *is* that thing on your arm?" Laney wrinkled her nose.

Noah groaned. "Are you seriously going to ask me all the exact same questions again?" he asked, not at all expecting an answer. "Look, we have to go now," he told her, gesturing toward the quantum shear.

Laney hesitated, looking between Noah and the conveniently person-sized, but ridiculously creepy and frightening, black hole before them. The dark gaping hole looked like a scream in her head. She felt chills all over again from the mere sight of the thing, as though for some reason, instinctively, she knew this wasn't going to end well for her.

He raised his eyebrows in a prompt. "Well? Come on."

"Where are we going?" she wanted to know, trying to stall, her heart pounding in her chest.

"It's going to be okay, Laney." He tried to reassure her. "All the answers you want—the explanations for all your hallucinations, why you can't remember anything, they're all right through there."

"H-how do I know that for sure?"

He pressed his hands to his face, frustrated. "Why is it so much harder to get you through the quantum shear this time? Is it because there's not a half-dead guy lying around who just tried to kill you?"

"A half-dead what?"

Noah rolled his eyes. "You just have to trust me."

"Trust you?" Laney echoed in a mocking tone. "I don't even know you! And you just go around kissing a girl you don't even know, who by the way, already has a boyfriend."

That irked him somewhat. "Hey," he began defensively. "The last time, you kissed *me* first! And I was engaged!"

"I did no such thing," she said haughtily, crossing her arms over her chest. "There's no way I would have done that."

He gritted his teeth in annoyance.

"I don't even believe it," she went on in disbelief. "How old are you anyway? *You*—have a fiancée?"

His face clouded over. "Not anymore."

Laney stopped, taken aback, and somehow, she sensed that she should stop that particular line of questioning immediately.

"Now, would you please just get in the damn black hole?" Noah insisted.

Laney motioned forward. "Why don't you go ahead?"

He tilted his head slightly. "Ladies first."

She let out a loud suffering, but resigned, groan. "Fiiiine." Then she took another deep breath. "Someone has a deeply twisted definition of chivalry," she muttered, before jumping into the swirling vortex of doom.

3

Parallel

Noah braced his hands on his knees, coughing.

Laney made a face. "Jeez, are you okay?" She was about to move to pat his back when she looked up to see where she was and her jaw dropped. "Holy shhh..."

The place was about as big as an airplane hangar, all gray and metal—certainly a stark contrast from the green, green quad gardens at her school.

About a dozen people wearing white lab coats and safety goggles were walking about, carefully stepping over cables on the floor as they came up to, and away from, several control panels, adjusting knobs and dials on the multitude of metal boxes arranged around a ginormous platform made of glass and mirrors in the middle of the room.

At first glance, the platform looked pretty daunting. That was until Laney noticed that it looked as though it—whatever *it* was—was only half-built, with several of its huge mirrored panels missing, or broken, or cracked.

Then she looked down at the ethereal blue light still shining up from underneath her and she noticed that the glass-and-mirrors platform she was currently standing on, set up in one far corner of the hangar, looked exactly like a smaller-scale replica of the ginormous one.

"Well, hell's bells, you made it."

Laney heard the voice from the sidelines and she turned slightly to see the person walk around to the front of their little platform.

"Laney, welcome back!" The guy with wheat blond hair and glasses greeted her with a grin. He was also, strangely, wearing a formal tie over a collarless woolly green sweater.

She shot him a weird look. "What?"

He kept smiling, as though proud. "You really don't remember, do you?"

Laney jumped slightly as the blue light of the platform flickered off and the loud humming stopped. She looked around again, bewildered, astounded. "Oh my god, this is really a parallel world, isn't it?" She glanced back down at Noah who was still bent down, seeming to be catching his breath, and wrinkled her nose, looking up at the other guy. "Is he going to be okay?" she asked.

The guy dismissed it with a wave. "He'll be fine. Quantum jumps usually have that effect, being that you basically just squeezed through a singularity, your entire body having been stretched apart at a subatomic level."

Laney looked down at herself. "I don't feel anything."

He grinned again. "You really don't, don't you?"

She narrowed her eyes at him as he was speaking to her like he knew her very well. "Do I know you?"

"Oh, sorry. I'm your assistant, Berry." He held out his hand to help her down off the platform. "Well, technically, I'm Dr. Laney Carter's assistant. The *other* Laney, from this dimension," he supplied.

She shot his hand a suspicious look, before looking around at some of the lab coats working in the room, many of whom seemed to be looking to him for instruction. She remarked, "You seem like you're more than just an assistant," as she stepped down.

"Well," Berry began. "I've sort of taken over as head of this lab since...well, um...since Laney uh...left." He glanced up at Noah, still on the platform. "Noah, you okay, man?"

Noah didn't answer right away. His hands were still braced on his knees, his head down.

"Hey, maybe you better get some rest," Berry suggested to him. "Nobody's been through that thing more than you have. You must be absolutely knackered."

"I'm fine," he spoke up, not looking up at them. "It's-it's actually not so bad anymore."

Laney looked from Berry to Noah and back to Berry again, her eyebrows raised, wondering if Berry would buy that. She barely knew him and she could already tell Noah was lying.

But before either Laney or Berry could say anything, Noah straightened up and stepped off the platform. "We've got work to do. This burned out again," he added, handing over a round little gadget to Berry.

Berry pursed his lips, pocketing the anchor device. "Alrighty." He shrugged in resignation. He called out several instructions to the lab coats standing by, all sounding like scientific gibberish to Laney, before he led the way out of the hangar. "Come this way."

Laney glanced back warily at Noah before following Berry. "Excuse me," she began as she caught up with Berry. "Hey, so what is this place?"

"This is GNR, Global Nuclear Research," Berry replied as they walked down the hallway. "It's the most advanced laboratory facility on Earth—that is, in our dimension. We work on ground-breaking research, mostly to do with quantum worlds and multiverses, and whatever else the cutting edge is on technology. And we also facilitate the remaining handful of military projects." He looked a bit uneasy. "We're still funded by the military branch of the government, but uh...let's just say, they've recently taken a step back to re-evaluate their involvement with regards to our scope of work."

Laney had paused by another large laboratory, as someone entered through the swinging double doors, allowing her a glimpse into the room, within which looked like there was a raging white-out blizzard, just seconds before the room lit up and entirely changed scenery to look like it was the middle of a scorching dry, sandy desert. "Wow." She breathed in awe.

Berry grinned at her reaction. "Don't get too attached. We're still undergoing major reconstruction in some parts of the lab. The uh...last administration left a lot of mess to clean up." He glanced back again to meet Noah's gaze. "And we're still cleaning it."

***

Noah didn't say anything as he followed behind Laney and Berry. The way Berry was talking made it all sound so simple but the last eight months had absolutely not been a piece of cake. At least not as far as Noah was concerned.

As if it wasn't enough that he'd had to deal with the political aftermath of thwarting the government-sponsored destruction of the multiverse eight months ago, there was, of course, the world-altering, significant, and irreversible loss of his fiancée, the *other* Laney.

And the feelings he'd had to struggle with were deeply strange, and in no uncertain terms, unbearable, since at the time, Noah had been working so hard for so long. He had been so focused on his mission of getting her back, that now that she was really gone, everything almost seemed pointless.

And then there was Laney. This Laney.

He watched her engrossed face as she listened to something that Berry was explaining and his chest tightened. He knew he definitely shouldn't have kissed her earlier, and inwardly, he was cursing himself. He had to make absolutely sure he didn't lose control like that again. He knew she didn't remember him. He knew she wasn't *his* Laney either.

But a Laney he did know was locked up in that mind. He hadn't even wanted to admit to himself until that morning how much he had been looking forward to seeing her again. *Her*. It was such an intense level-up in the severity of confusing, it was bordering on ridiculous.

The three of them arrived at the door to a big office with floor-to-ceiling glass windows that looked out to the busy lobby of the facility.

Berry placed his hand on the panel beside the door and

it lit up green as the door opened. "Sorry about the mess," he said as they all walked into the office.

Laney raised her eyebrows, noting, "It looks like my dorm room."

Stacks and stacks of half-unpacked boxes everywhere, with several blackboards and whiteboards lining the walls, books, papers, and strange contraptions piled high on tables, on chairs, and on the floor, an odd stack of orange traffic cones was haphazardly strewn in one corner.

"Sure." She shrugged nonchalantly as she walked up to the big windows to watch the people bustling outside. She glanced back over at Noah, easily meeting his gaze as she had noticed—had been *acutely* aware that he had been staring at her since they had left the jump platform.

But Noah just looked away.

Laney chewed on her bottom lip.

He'd said she knew him. It must have been absolutely nerve-wracking for her to think about how he could possibly know her when she couldn't even remember anything about him. Especially since he even believed he knew her well enough to kiss her this morning.

From the look in her eyes, he could tell she was thinking about it too. The hairs on the back of his neck stood up at the memory. Not because it had felt good. But because it had felt really, really, *ridiculously*, really good.

She seemed to shake her head to clear the thought and let out a sigh as she regarded the two guys with a look. "So," she started. "Not to bring up the giant elephant in the room, but why am I here—'again' allegedly?" she added skeptically.

"Well," Berry said. "I'm not sure how much Noah has told you about what's going on—"

Laney raised her eyebrows at him before shooting Noah a cursory glance. "Somehow I get the feeling he's not much of a talker."

Berry chuckled under his breath. "Okay, then maybe let's start from the beginning." He waved his hand ceremoniously. "About eight months ago, you crossed over to this world with Noah through a quantum shear—"

She blinked. "Why?" she wanted to know.

Berry shot Noah a cautious look before uneasily meeting Laney's gaze again. "Um...maybe let's put a pin in that first, shall we?"

Laney had a hint of puzzlement on her face, but then just gestured for him to continue. "If you say so."

"Uh, anyway," Berry went on. "You got hit by an energy beam just as you tried to enter the quantum shear—"

"An energy beam, what, like from a weapon?" Laney prompted.

"Yes."

"What, someone shot me? Who? Why?"

Berry wrinkled his nose, looking over at Noah again. "Um, let me get back to that."

Laney frowned. "It doesn't sound like you're actually telling me anything."

"It's not really relevant to your current situation," Noah interjected.

She turned to glare at him. "How about I decide that?"

"Guys! Please." Berry put up his hands. Then he sighed. "How about I just jump right to it." He looked over at Laney.

"Basically, on that first jump that you made with Noah eight months ago, you got hit by an energy beam just as you tried to enter a quantum shear."

Laney raised her eyebrows in a prompt.

"Well, first of all, it destabilized your jump calibrations," Berry relayed. "Which was by the way, why you and he got separated when you first arrived in this world. But most importantly, it caused your entire atomic structure to phase."

She gave him a blank, pointed look. "Uh...what?"

Berry pursed his lips. "To be honest, we were hoping that you had somehow avoided the full brunt of the blast and that it wouldn't come to this and that someone should have told me sooner—"

Clearing his throat uncomfortably, Noah looked away to avoid Berry's pointed gaze.

But Berry turned back to Laney in resignation. "But you've been...detached, from your original world—uprooted, as it were. And now, your other parallel world selves are bleeding through you."

He tilted his head meaningfully. "It means your hallucinations—what you've been experiencing, is an apparent shifting between a random selection of your other selves, inhabiting them, sometimes inheriting their characteristics, their personalities, gaining some of their memories." He paused. "I think Noah mentioned it's already started happening. And unfortunately, it's going to keep happening. Until the actual 'you' eventually fades away into uh..." He cleared his throat, uneasy. "Nothing."

Laney took a deep breath.

But the true gravity of the situation didn't quite seem to

be settling in with her yet. And aside from the strange dreams and hallucinations, she would have had no gauge as to how serious the problem actually was. She couldn't even remember any of it to begin with. Noah could even guess Laney might still think she was merely dreaming.

She just shrugged again. "And I suppose you know how to fix it?"

"Well, no," Berry replied with another frown before his eyes lit up. "But I've been working on it, and I've come to a crucial point. That's sort of why I asked Noah to go get you."

Laney met Noah's gaze again for a moment but her wary, questioning eyes were making him uncomfortable. He turned to stare out the big window, folding his arms across his chest.

Berry waved his hand again. "Either way, I don't think it's safe for you to go back to your original world until this is all sorted," he told her. "Your doctors or...scientists over there definitely won't be equipped to deal with your particularly...unique situation."

"So, what—I'm like, stuck here?" Laney moaned.

"Actually, quite the opposite," Berry rationalized. "You're displaced. You're not stuck anywhere."

She frowned again. "But my friends, my parents—I have finals this week. I'll never get a chance to make it up before I graduate."

Noah and Berry exchanged odd looks.

"Graduate?" Berry repeated the word.

"Yeah, graduate, you know—move on from high school to college, or whatever," Laney explained. "What, you guys don't have school here?"

"Yes, of course, but we don't *graduate*," Berry relayed.

"We all just go to school, do an apprenticeship, and then eventually settle straight into a career based on our aptitude. Besides," he rationalized. "I think it would be pretty pointless to have to mark each occasion whenever we would level-up a school year. It would happen too frequently."

Laney shot him a curious look. "Why?"

"Because our brains age faster, remember? Caused by the —oh right, you don't remember uh..." Berry shook his head before he relayed as though it was no big deal whatsoever, "Sixty-seven years ago, nearly all organic life on our world was obliterated by a global cascade bomb."

"*W-what*?" Laney gasped in shock, horrified. Then she paused. "Wait, then how come you all are still here? And shouldn't we be worried about like radiation or something?"

Noah rolled his eyes, having heard all this before.

"No, no." Berry shook his head again. "That's not exactly— you know what?" He stopped short, his eyes lighting up. "I have a clip you can watch."

Laney shot him a skeptical look. "You do?"

4

For Real

Berry was rummaging through several boxes in his office, looking for something.

He cleared a stack of papers off a control board on the table and made a face. "Dude, at some point, you've really got to get rid of some of this stuff," he told Noah, picking up several books and contraptions to show him before he fished out a little metal box with a single red light indicator, which was hooked up to the control panel and began to unplug it to put it out of the way.

Noah snapped. "No!"

Laney looked up, surprised at his outburst.

Berry stopped short.

"This is Laney's stuff. We're leaving everything as it is," Noah said, his tone firm.

Berry gave him a meaningful look but didn't say anything else. He just went on to scour the mess for something. "There has to be something here—," he went on mumbling. "I'm pretty sure I had a—aha!" He had unearthed what looked like an old film reel.

Berry walked across the room and dragged something out of a dark corner. It was a filmstrip viewer mounted on a squeaky old roller cart.

Then he slipped the film reel in, pressed a few buttons, and an old video crackled against a white screen on the wall.

He turned to Laney. "Well, this actually shows the population migration after the cascade bomb event, but it's pretty informative."

Cautious, Laney seemed to brace herself as she watched the vintage-filtered black-and-white video.

It showed an image of the globe turning counter-clockwise slowly. After a moment, a pin dropped onto the continental U.K., zooming in and landing on London, right before a giant explosion blew across the continent.

Noah didn't have to look. He had seen the film multiple times. It was taught in their schools as part of their history. It was just plain fact. But the look of uncontained shock, of horror, of bewilderment on Laney's face as she absorbed the content was intriguing.

He narrowed his eyes. In her world, the cascade bomb had never happened. Life had simply moved on and everything was normal. But before Noah could even consider wondering what "normal" was like, he quickly dismissed the thought.

There was no point in thinking about what could have been.

"Holy cow..." Laney breathed.

Noah glanced up to see that she was remarking on the

casualty count being displayed on the screen, but he didn't flinch. To him, it wasn't just a movie, it wasn't make-believe, and he already knew how it ended.

Laney on the other hand, couldn't tear her gaze away from the screen.

Several arrows appeared, flashing in indication of movement from Africa and Europe, as those continents were engulfed by a dark cloud before the cloud moved to cover America and Asia as well.

She frowned at the continuous flickering display of casualty numbers as they were all in the hundreds of millions —and indeed depressing. Instead, she was focused on the arrows. They were all headed downward.

Then the globe spun again to show the complete opposite side of the world from London and another pin dropped on the lower part of the northern island of the little country right at the bottom of the world—a place where the dark cloud had not quite managed to reach, where all the arrows converged.

The end of the film in the reel clicked as it spun around the projector dial.

Berry reached over to flip the switch off before turning to Laney. "Did you understand?"

She spoke slowly. "Ssooo...some type of massive bomb killed this whole planet and everyone who didn't die moved down to that bottom country?"

"Exactly!" Berry grinned, looking pleased. "In the past few decades, even though some areas of the world have re-generated in terms of biodiversity, only certain parts have been repopulated," he relayed. "Most of them serve as science stations, or outposts tasked by the government to retrieve specific resources. Some places have been restored, mainly because it would be a major feat to reconstruct its infrastructure elsewhere. Like this place." He gestured around them before going on. "But in terms of people density, the numbers haven't quite recovered enough to warrant building settlements elsewhere."

Laney swallowed hard as though the image of the dark cloud engulfing the entire Earth was still vivid in her mind. "This is so terrible..."

"It's just history," Noah spoke up, his tone clipped, taking her reaction as criticism against his world, instead of compassion. "This is *our* reality. *Our* world. We didn't have a choice in the matter but we're doing the best we can with it. And maybe instead of judging us, you need to contemplate how you're taking *your* world for granted."

Laney sighed, shooting a pleading look toward Berry. "Dear god, does he have a muzzle?"

Berry covered his mouth with his hand, stifling his chuckle.

But after a moment, Laney just rolled her eyes. "So, okay," she started. "Now that I've been shocked to death—in addition to being sufficiently freaked out, what's next?"

Berry spoke up. "First things first. We have to get your memory back. Dr. Chambers, I mentioned her to you once before. She specializes in the research into the biological and genetic changes brought about by the global cascade bomb. But she's also a neuroscientist," he explained. "I'd been working with her on the serum that we used to make you forget your time here last time. So you'll have to go and get the anti-serum from her. She runs her lab out of Wellington."

"Wellington," she echoed. "Is it far? Where the hell are we anyway?"

Berry crossed over to his desk and spun a silver metal globe on his table and pointed to Switzerland. "We are here." Then he spun it again, to the absolute opposite side, to point. "Wellington is here."

Laney blew out a breath. "Whoa. It has to be at the other end of the world, doesn't it?" She squinted to read the words on the globe. "New...Zealand. I think I've heard of it."

Berry nodded. "Yes, which is why you should leave as soon as possible. The fastest airship leaves tonight. But first, I'll need to run some tests, take some samples, DNA, blood," he said, moving to check the console on his desk for reference. "So I can work on figuring out how to fix your displacement problem from here. I'll need to stay behind and look after the rehabilitation of the lab, to make sure everything stays on track."

"Really?" Laney looked puzzled, but before she could ask her question, Berry answered it.

"But Noah will take you."

She met Noah's gaze and made a face, repeating in distaste, "Really?"

Noah's eyebrows rose in irritated slight.

Berry stifled his chuckle again, glancing over at him. "Don't worry. It's a commuter airship, so you won't be alone. And I'll be on the radio if you need to talk to me. I'll have to keep you posted on my progress for your cure anyway."

"I don't suppose I have much of a choice, do I?"

"Uh, no, not really," Berry told Laney with a small grin.

"Let me just go get my kit from my old lab. You can wait here in this office."

He moved to leave before he stopped short of Noah as though he remembered something. "Oh, one thing." He glanced up at him tentatively. "Uh...I was going to tell you. I mean, I thought I should let you know. My preliminary results indicated that the effects of the cure would be irreversible."

"Meaning?" Laney overheard from across the room and drawled her prompt, sounding almost bored.

"Meaning...if we actually manage to root you back to your original world," Berry began, flicking a glance over at Noah again, before meeting Laney's gaze. "You'll no longer be able to stand the stresses of a quantum jump thereafter, or perhaps not even be able to perceive anything extra-dimensionally any longer."

Noah met her gaze, an unreadable expression on his face.

"Why does he do that?" Laney asked Noah, looking puzzled again. "I didn't understand a single word he said."

Noah took a deep breath. "He means—you'll never see us again."

She threw up her hands. "Thank god! When do we start this curing thing?"

Noah looked over at Berry again, his face sullen.

Berry just made a show of shrugging. "You guys just wait here. I'll be right back," he said, turning to go, but Noah stopped him just outside the room.

"Hey, it feels like she's a completely different person again," Noah said under his breath, so Laney couldn't hear. "Are you sure this is the right Laney?"

Berry replied, looking bemused. "I thought *you* would know."

Noah visibly clenched his jaw again.

Berry noticed, a faint smirk appearing on his face. "So you've kissed her again, huh?"

Noah just glared at him for a moment, before turning away.

"That's a yes," Berry quipped.

Noah watched as Laney looked around the office which used to be Eleanor's. She was peering at certain objects on the tables and shelves curiously.

It was a bit strange to watch for Noah as, despite appearances, here was Laney, alive and well, back in her own office, inspecting a framed magazine cover with a stylized portrait of herself on it, beside her own framed Nobel Prize plaque.

Awarded to Dr. Eleanor Carter.
For outstanding breakthroughs in
the pursuit of the understanding
of the multiverse.

"Wow," Laney breathed as she read the inscription. "That other Laney's some kind of super-genius, huh?"

"She certainly liked to think so," Noah said.

She shot him a brief amused look at the phrasing of his reply.

"Eleanor was the one who made all the discoveries to make

it possible to cross into other dimensions. It was her life's work," Noah relayed. "None of this would even be happening if it wasn't for her."

At that last statement, Laney caught his expression change. It was subtle, but regardless of the regret in his tone, Noah was sure he couldn't keep the pride out of his voice.

"Eleanor," she repeated, as she looked around the room. "Suits her," she said. "Certainly more than it suits me," she added in a slightly mocking manner.

Then her gaze fell on a framed photo on the table.

A photo of Eleanor and Noah.

And her jaw dropped. "Whoa. She totally looks exactly like me." Then she stopped, straightening up to meet his gaze as she realized something. "You were engaged to her."

Noah narrowed his eyes, only slightly surprised that she had already figured that out. "Yes."

"Ohhh!" She slapped her palm to her forehead. "*That's* why you kissed me."

Noah's forehead creased upon hearing the relief in her voice.

Then Laney made a face, in sympathy. "You must miss her a lot then, huh? What happened to her?"

Noah stiffened. "I don't want to talk about it."

"Right...of course." Laney rolled her eyes.

And then she reared her arm back to swing her fist right at his face.

5

The Bleed

Berry heard a crash coming from around the corner as he walked back to the big office, carrying his lab kit. His forehead creased as he walked faster, skidding to a stop outside the open office door just as Noah commando-rolled out of it.

"Noah?" he prompted, watching in disbelief as Noah jumped to brace himself flat against the wall beside the doorway. "What's going—?"

Noah cut him off, grabbing his sweater, just in time to pull him back from the path of a large metal stapler having been hurtled out the doorway.

"Whoa!" Berry exclaimed as he stood behind Noah, pressing against the wall himself. "Holy heck, are you bleeding?" he gasped, only then noticing that Noah had bleeding cuts on his lip and his eyebrow, looking as though he had just come out of a fight.

Noah's eyebrows were furrowed as he heaved, sneaking furtive glances into the office.

"You're disrupting my mission again, Donovan!" Laney's voice hissed out, and several more unidentified heavy things crashed inside the office before a coffee mug smashed against the wall outside.

"Jeez!" Berry's eyes widened in shock. "What the hell is Laney doing in there?"

"That's not freaking Laney!" Noah told him.

"What?" Berry looked confused. "How do you know?"

"I just—I just do, alright?" Noah replied, still trying to catch his breath. "She's phased or something. I think it's one of her alternate selves bleeding through."

"One that just so happens to want to kill you?"

"Yes."

"Well, technically, the other one wanted to kill you too, but just not this way."

"Alright, thanks, it's hilarious." He rubbed his bruised jaw, looking annoyed as hell. "It feels like she's also trained in Special Forces, like she knew every move I was going to make before I made it."

Just then, an ornate silver metal letter opener whizzed past Noah's head before it lodged halfway into the wall across the doorway.

"Uh-oh," Berry started, wrinkling his nose. "I think she's found—"

"Please tell me you don't collect letter openers," Noah cut in his warning.

Berry gave him a wan smile, just as three more fancy-looking letter openers shot through the doorway like arrows, one of them smashing to pieces on the tile floor. "Oh man, not my antique ivory one!" He groaned. "I lifted that from a poacher down in—"

Noah shot him a look of disbelief. "Berry!" he snapped, giving him an expectant look.

"Oh, right." Berry nodded. He stretched out his hand past Noah, to enter a code into the door's touch panel to trigger the "intruder alert" inside the office.

They heard a soft beep and a loud fizzle, just before they heard Laney moan and then fall to the floor, unconscious.

Noah was bent down at Laney's eye level, watching intently as her eyes began to flutter open.

She met his gaze, feeling dazed. "Noah...?" she asked, her eyes instantly widening in alarm as she realized that she was strapped down to a chair in a small examination room, and she struggled in panic. "What the hell is going on? Why am I tied down?"

Noah watched her face for another moment before he glanced up at Berry. "She's back."

Berry let out a sigh of relief. "Thank god," he said, pressing a button on the console behind him, which instantly released the clamps holding Laney's wrists and ankles to the chair.

"It's okay, Laney." Noah took her hands to help her up, his forehead creasing as he noticed she was still shaking from panic, but he just swallowed hard and stepped back. "Sorry about that. You weren't quite yourself."

"Did I...Was I someone else?"

Noah nodded.

Laney noticed the cuts on his face and her jaw dropped. "Oh my god, *I* did that—to *you*?" she asked, even as her tone sounded more amused, almost pleased, rather than aghast.

And Berry chuckled. "You were totally kicking his ass," he remarked.

Laney cracked a grin.

Noah shook his head. "I'm glad you're all amused."

Berry was still grinning. "All kidding aside, we probably need to monitor all these 'bleed throughs' more closely, in case one of your random personalities goes apples and bananas out of control again."

She raised her eyebrows. "What do you mean?"

"This." Berry held up a little opaque strip closer to her face. "It's a cerebral cortex link. It'll track your brain activity for any anomalies...and..." He hesitated.

She blinked expectantly. "And?"

Berry didn't reply.

Laney glanced up at Noah instead. "And?"

Noah pursed his lips before spelling it out. "And it could be programmed to deliver a sharp jolt to your system, in case we need to incapacitate you again."

Laney blew out a breath sharply. "Huh."

Noah tilted his head slightly as he regarded her with a look. "You can say no. We're not going to force you to wear it."

She paused, seeming to be thinking about it, then her eyes moved to the cut on his mouth, and as she averted her gaze. "I don't want to hurt anyone else."

Berry glanced up at Noah as if seeking his approval first. Then he just shrugged and reached over to attach the little strip behind Laney's ear.

"Ow." Laney winced, making a face as the strip bonded to her skin.

Berry let out a sigh. "Well, now that all the excitement is over," he began. "I better get those samples quickly or you're going to miss your flight."

She nodded and sat back down again toward where Berry gestured as he pulled an instrument table closer. She glanced over at Noah who had gone to stand by the door. "I don't think I've ever had that happen before. I had absolutely no idea what I was doing," she said, turning to Berry. "The...hallucinations in the past, I've always been completely aware of them, and aware that they weren't real. And I had no idea any one of my alternate world selves could possibly do *that*." She motioned her chin in the direction of Noah's face.

"Well," Berry began, even as he worked. "You know the nature of the multiverse is exactly that. It means anything that can happen, will, or already has happened, in at least *one* parallel world, and there could be billions upon billions of permutations and quantum worlds and alternate selves."

Laney screwed up her face, as the incident had just sorely driven home the gravity of her situation, and it dawned on her what it actually meant when Berry had said that she could potentially lose herself, as if any of her alternate selves decided to stay, *she* definitely would fade away into nothing. She swallowed hard.

"Have you been having weird dreams in the past few months?" Berry asked.

"To say the least."

"About what?"

"Well," she started slowly. "Different things, different

places. Sometimes I'm in the middle of a busy city, and sometimes I'm up a mountain in the middle of nowhere."

She narrowed her eyes in recall. "Now that I think about it, I'm pretty sure I've dreamt about that giant platform thingy back there a few times. But it's like...when I've seen things happen over and over again, each time something is slightly different." She looked up at Berry. "That must be what you meant by the billions of permutations, huh?"

He nodded. "You know, Laney was in the middle of an experiment where she postulated that dreaming was actually an artifact of a 'bleed through'. You know how you always dream that you're falling, or being chased or something? She reckoned you were possibly seeing through the eyes of another you, in another dimension."

Laney's eyes were glazed over as she absorbed the information. "Fascinating..."

Berry shot Noah another amused look at her use of the expression before he shrugged to go on. "Except, of course, you don't usually remember what happened when you wake up the next morning."

"And they definitely shouldn't be manifesting when I'm wide awake and taking over my consciousness altogether," Laney supplied.

"That's right." Berry nodded. "But because of Eleanor's experiment, your delta and alpha waves might still be all muddled up from last time."

Laney tilted her head, taking a moment to absorb Berry's last statement. "Eleanor's what?" she asked in disbelief. "Did you just say the other Laney was doing some kind of experiment on *my* brain waves?"

"Uh…" Berry blinked, flustered.

"Eleanor did a lot of things," Noah spoke up, in Eleanor's defense. "Some things she wasn't proud of, but part of science is pushing the boundaries. She may have done some morally questionable things in the past, but she believed what she was doing was for the betterment of the whole world."

Laney met his gaze, frowning slightly.

Noah never seemed to show as much emotion as whenever he spoke about Eleanor. She wasn't even here and he was protecting her stuff, protecting her memory. And for a crazy split second, Laney felt envious of Eleanor.

It might have been obvious, being that they *were* intending to get married, but she could tell that he really loved her—*still* really loved her.

"Oh, look who's here to see you!" Berry announced, the wide grin on his face absolutely betraying his total relief for the timely interruption.

Laney followed his gaze expectantly, but her gaze stopped short at the empty doorway, not seeing what he was referring to. "What? Who are you talking about?"

Then she heard two chirps coming from beneath her and she looked down to see a little metal robot, its gears and spokes visible from the outside, running on three-wheeled little treads. She looked blankly at the robot. "Do I know…it?"

Berry smiled. "His name is P.T.," he told her. "You guys had gone on some adventures the last time you were here."

"Oh."

The little robot chirped again and it appeared to tilt its "head", or whatever the front section of its mechanism was, looking up at her curiously.

"Oh." Berry was looking at the robot before he looked up at Laney again. "He wants to come with you. I think he really likes you," he whispered with a grin, leaning closer to her.

"Um, I'm flattered...?"

"P.T.'s had some upgrades. I'm sure he'll come in handy again," Berry told her.

She chuckled, amused, as she watched P.T. do spinning circles on the floor. "If you say so."

Then Berry blew out a breath. "There." He zipped up the last sample bag with a satisfied nod. "I should have enough to work with for now, with this, plus the data from your CCL—"

"My what?"

"That." Berry pointed to the strip behind her ear. "I'll be monitoring your readings from my lab, but it'll also ping Noah's HUD if there are any irregularities with your brain waves—not that he wouldn't have already noticed if you start suddenly kicking down doors or throwing people against windows." He attempted the joke, glancing up at Noah who was already fiddling with his HUD to make sure the gadget was all synched up.

Laney looked unenthused. "Fun."

"I don't think I have to tell you, Noah, but you do know time is of the essence," Berry said loudly, making sure Noah met his pointed look.

"When is it ever not?" Noah replied, already looking bothered before he glanced over at Laney with an unveiled condescending look. "Do you think you could possibly keep that in mind so that we can deliver you to Dr. Chambers as expediently as possible?"

"Fine." She rolled her eyes. "Then let's go see this amazing brain doctor, and see if she can't shrink my head and wake me up from this obvious nightmare..." she trailed off as she walked out the door first, with P.T. zipping suit at her heels.

Noah watched the two of them head away with a slight shake of his head.

Berry smirked, his shoulders shaking. He patted Noah's shoulder once. "Good luck, man."

6

The Community

Laney didn't know how long they had been flying for, except that the sky outside the airship vessel windows was purple.

It was still dusk. Or rather, it was dusk again.

"Are we there yet?" she asked as she felt the airship dip in descent.

Noah glanced out the window from beside her. "No, they're just breaking the trip in half to reload the burners, because it's such a long way to go."

Laney had never been on a hot air balloon before, but she figured it was probably the closest thing to riding in the giant commuter airship that she was on, except that the airship was somehow incredibly fast.

She looked out the window, up at the massive silver-bronze envelope lit underneath by several burners, which enabled the gondola vessel structure to float in the air, then glanced down at the shadows of the spinning propellers in the back against the smattering of clouds in the sky beneath them.

P.T. was perched on the backrest of the bench seat and when Laney straightened up to look out the window, it rolled closer to the windows as well, as though to look outside itself.

On the horizon, Laney saw a row of low colonial-style-columned buildings along the waterfront of what looked like a flat urban area, but upon closer inspection, and even in the dusk light, she could see that the entire place looked more like a jungle, with overgrown forests that had spilled onto the roadways and encroaching over ruins of city structures further inland.

The airship was coming down toward a concrete strip that jutted out from the main island. It was probably where the airship was going to dock to refuel.

"What is this place?" she asked, feeling the humid air against her skin as the airship descended, as though they had flown into a layer of hot atmosphere.

Noah replied, "It used to be a British colony called Singapore. We're very near the equator. That's why it's suddenly warmer."

Laney's eyebrows rose up. "Really?" She was no geography buff, but she was pretty sure that Singapore was a country in its own right. Then again, maybe all that would only have happened if the cascade bomb hadn't torn the entire world apart. "Wow. I bet it would be just fascinating to compare how small or how big the differences are between our worlds since our histories deviated sixty-seven years ago," she mused aloud.

At that, Noah glanced over and she met his gaze. It looked

as though he wanted to say something more, but instead, he reached down to retrieve his jacket, which had been bundled up for Laney to sleep on earlier, to hang it up on a wall peg, before standing up.

"I'll go get some food," he said and turned to walk away.

Laney was puzzled at his bizarre response but dismissed it. She looked over at P.T. "So? Are you having fun so far?" she asked with a slightly mocking tone, as of course, she was trying to communicate with a "robot". It was like trying to talk to a paperweight on wheels.

"Berry said we went on some adventures together last time," she said. "I don't suppose you can tell me what happened back then, can you?"

P.T. just squeaked and chirped, spinning his wheels.

She shook her head. "No? Yeah, didn't think so."

Noah came back with two bottles of chocolate-flavored whey protein and he held one out to her. "I figured you actually haven't had any food since lunch yesterday."

"Well, since before lunch," Laney corrected. "You actually dropped in *during* my lunch break." He gave her a pointed look and she supplied the reply he was waiting for, "But thanks." She took a big gulp before asking, "How much longer until we get there?"

"We still have a few more hours to go if you want to rest some more."

Laney made a face. She had managed to get a few hours of sleep earlier, only to be woken up, gasping and panicking. Not even being in this strange parallel world could cure her of her vivid, scary nightmares. And the thought of going to sleep only to have those nightmares again was not at all appealing to her. "Maybe I'll just take a little stroll outside and watch the ship land," she said, starting to stand.

Noah caught her arm. "I'm—not sure that's a good idea."

She shrugged him off, rolling her eyes as she pulled on the fur-collared vintage trench coat that Berry had found for her to wear so she could blend in easier with the population. "I think it's a safe bet I'm not going to get lost in this airship. *Also*, I wasn't asking for your permission," she pointed out. "*Also*, I can take care of myself."

He gave her an even look. "Can you? And who's going to take care of all these innocent people when one of your alternate selves bleeds through again? Particularly G.I. Janey?"

Laney sighed. "Look, if I phase again, feel free to zap me."

Noah did not look satisfied, but he knew full well he wasn't going to win this one. "Fine. Then take P.T. with you, just in case."

She shot him a weird look. "Just in case what? Just in case the little robot can tackle me to the ground if I start attacking people?" she mocked before she stopped short. "Wait, can it actually do that?" she asked cautiously.

P.T. spun its wheels, chirping on the window, in response.

Noah gave her an exasperated look. "Just in case you need to call *me* for help," he supplied.

Laney huffed. "Fine," she said. "Somehow, I don't think it wants to stay here with you anyway," she added with a smirk, picking up the robot, before moving toward the door of the cabin to head outside.

***

After only a few minutes, Noah craned his neck to check on Laney. He saw her on the airship deck with P.T. on her shoulder. Laney was already animatedly chatting up a dark-haired girl, who had come aboard at the same time as several other new passengers from Singapore.

Noah clenched his jaw as he looked out the window toward the horizon, thinking about Eleanor again, since if she hadn't been such an immoral scientific genius, he would have never even attempted to cross into the other world, and he would have never met *this* Laney.

There wouldn't be any unnecessary complications to this mission, and he would just be doing her a service, like the unaffected neutral party protective detail he was supposed to be. He couldn't even begin to imagine how simple his life would have been had that been the case.

And in some alternate world, it probably was.

Several little signs mounted on the cabin ceiling clicked, switching from saying 'ARRIVED' to 'DEPARTING'. A loud whistle blew outside to indicate that the airship was about to take off again.

Noah was looking up toward the deck to make sure Laney was heading back into the cabin, when he felt a prickly sensation in the back of his neck, as though he was being watched himself. He narrowed his eyes, looking around trying to spot anything suspicious nearby.

But all he could see was a cabin full of people, all weary-looking, either jostling for a seat or being already seated upon rows and rows of benches, eager for the airship to reach its destination.

Then when he glanced up again, Laney was no longer on the ship's deck.

In fact, he could no longer see her anywhere.

He sat up, alerted, looking around furtively again, the slight crease of concern on his forehead easily seconds away from turning into a full-blown worry frown.

He had already lost one Laney. He was absolutely not ready to lose another.

Noah stood up, swallowing hard. But just as the crowd parted, he finally spotted Laney inside. He took a deep breath, belatedly realizing that his heart had already started to pound in alarm.

She was still talking to the dark-haired girl, but they were standing near the windows across the indoor cabin, amongst a new group of other people.

Noah frowned slightly, lowering back down in his seat.

He was a little bit concerned with how the people from this world would treat Laney, being that "Dr. Laney Carter" was a household name, and there was definitely no mistaking the resemblance.

But Laney was laughing at something and she fist-bumped one of the other guys in the group. Although Noah was too far away to hear what they were talking about. Then a blonde guy beside Laney casually slung his arm around her shoulders.

Noah blinked, instantly pushing off.

***

"Who is that?"

"Who?" Laney glanced up toward whom Rui, the dark-haired girl, was referring, in time to see Noah striding toward them from across the cabin. She met his gaze briefly as he threw his heavy flight jacket back on, his T-shirt stretching across his chest.

"*That*," Rui replied, her mouth nearly dropping open.

Laney's gaze was distracted.

She noticed a couple of groups of other young girls whom Noah passed by turn their heads to watch him brush past, before giggling to themselves. *He must love that*, she thought to herself in disbelief.

Not that she could blame them.

Noah's demeanor was definitely a far cry from the chatty, arrogant air that was Jake Donovan, but he was just as hot—or probably even more so—with his usually slicked-back black hair all tousled and unruly.

But Laney just groaned to herself. It's like it wasn't hard enough that she was in a freaky alternate world where she had only met two people so far, she couldn't even take five minutes to talk to some other kids and feel semi-normal again before the most anti-social babysitter ever came along to ruin everything.

"He looks pissed off," Simon, the guy standing to Rui's other side, commented.

Laney rolled her eyes. "That's just Noah," she said. "He always looks pissed off."

"Laney," Noah called out as he arrived.

The urgency in his tone made her worry. "Noah, what's wrong?" she asked, alerted.

But Noah just cleared his throat. "Sorry to interrupt," he said, looking around at the rest of the group, his gaze settling on the blonde guy beside Laney for a moment, who instantly drew back.

"Oh shit, is he the primary?" Simon turned to Rui to ask under his breath.

Laney overheard and shot him a strange look. "The what?"

But in Noah's presence, the guys all seemed eager to disperse.

"Hey Rui, we're just going to go find our seats," Simon bade her as the rest of the group scrambled away with only awkward farewells. "Catch you later. It was nice to meet you, Laney." He mocked a salute at her before walking away himself.

And in no time at all, Laney was left standing with only Rui and Noah.

Laney looked around, confused. "What just happened?"

Rui simply chuckled, before putting her hand out for Noah. "Hi, I'm Dr. Rui Minato."

At that, Laney snapped to alert. "Oh! Sorry, Noah, this is Rui." She began introductions. "She's a dendrogeologenetical scientist. She's studying some of the tropical forests here in Singapore."

Noah's eyebrows rose. "You mean, a dendrological geneticist."

Laney wrinkled her nose. "You know, you can let some of them go," she told Noah. "I'm obviously the dumbest girl on this planet. You don't have to advertise it."

Rui laughed again. "I'm sorry," she said to Noah. "I didn't have the heart to correct her. I was an avid reader of her papers. Yours too. Quantum physics would have been my second choice of specialty."

"Uh...thanks," Noah mumbled, not quite seeming to know how to respond to the compliment. Then he asked Laney in a low voice, "Did you tell all these people who you are?"

But Rui herself nodded. "Oh, don't worry. My team was at GNR a few months ago and we'd all heard about the other parallel world's Laney. The one that was not a scientist."

Laney raised her hand. "Present," she said, looking almost apologetic.

Rui giggled. "I can't even imagine how strange you must think this world is. How different."

P.T. spun his wheels with a screech as if to punctuate her statement.

And Laney laughed, nodding. "Yes. I'd have to say I honestly haven't stopped being amazed since I arrived here."

Noah gave her a pointed warning look and her smile faded a bit before she went on. "Although, I am looking forward to seeing what this new country of yours is like." She turned to Noah briefly. "Rui was just telling me about The Community and about cultural preservation."

Then she turned to Rui to speak a long flurry of fluent Japanese before ending with a prompt, "*desshou?*"

"*Sou!*" Rui replied with a smile. She looked up at Noah. "I was telling Laney that we take preservation very seriously in our world, being that a significant portion of the world's culture had been completely wiped out—some of which can never be recovered. It's a rarity nowadays to find speakers of other languages. Everyone just speaks English. I mean, I barely get to practice speaking myself," she admitted before turning to Laney again. "But *you* are amazing!"

Laney gave her a self-effacing *oh-stop* wave.

Rui turned to Noah. "She speaks Japanese like she actually lived in Japan. It's incredible!"

Noah met Laney's gaze evenly. "Well, that does indeed sound amazing," he said with a catch in his tone as though he couldn't wait to wrap up the conversation and Laney made another face.

Rui looked from one to the other, as though herself sensing that Noah was eager to conclude their interaction, and she managed an uncomfortable smile. "Well, I suppose I better go re-join my team. It was truly an honor to meet you, Laney."

"Hey, it was great to meet you too, Rui." Laney gave her a little bow. "*Ja, mata ne!*"

"*Mata ne!*" Rui said with a smile, before turning to walk away.

7

The Line

"So what, you speak Japanese now, too?" Noah asked when Laney met his gaze again, and she just shrugged. "But you're still yourself." He peered at her face, then glanced down discreetly at his HUD to double-check the status of her CCL.

"I guess being a linguist doesn't require overtaking my entire consciousness."

"Good." Noah looked satisfied. "We're trying to keep you on the down-low. I'm assuming you knew better than to be telling those people about the differences between your world and ours? At least one big one in particular?"

Laney sighed. "Would you give me a little credit?"

"I just did," he pointed out. "In any case, I don't think it's a good idea for you to be socializing with too many people here. You know this isn't your world."

She rubbed the bridge of her nose, exasperated. "Yes, yes, you don't have to keep rubbing it in. I am glaringly aware of the fact." She shook her head. "No offense, but given that this was actually Eleanor's world, you know, the '*Super Genius*', I was sort of expecting them—" She jerked her thumb in the direction of Rui's team. "To be a lot more broken up about her being gone."

Noah's jaw clenched. He let out a sigh, turning to lean against the railing by the windows to look outside. "That's because they don't know what really happened."

"They don't?" Laney looked puzzled. "Hey, I know *I* just don't remember, but how could *they* not even know?"

"GNR is about an entire world away from The Community," he told her. "And there's already enough friction between GNR and certain sectors of society. Some people are still not happy about even the mere existence of the *Quantum Jump Project*. The President decided that any more bad press about the program or the lab wasn't going to do anyone any good."

"But you don't agree," Laney stated, leaning forward herself to read his face, as she put P.T. down on the windowsill.

"Whatever." Noah shrugged. "They just wanted people to move on with their lives. Maybe sometimes, science should...just stay theoretical, you know?" He ran his hand through his hair roughly. "I don't know anymore. There are times I wish we'd never even made those breakthroughs. But other times..." He paused, looking at her. "I can't even imagine not having made them."

Laney pursed her lips. She supposed it also hurt Noah even just to talk about Eleanor. But she averted her gaze, straightening up. "Well, if you ask me," she started, trying to be upbeat. "I think scientific discoveries should be made with consideration of their consequences. You know, Jurassic Park was all over it."

A corner of Noah's mouth tilted up in amusement. "You said that last time, too. Although, I didn't get the reference at the time either."

"Really?" she asked, chuckling under her breath. "Well then, this must be very strange to you—having all these conversations all over again with me."

"Well...we really didn't have much time for conversation last time."

Laney's smile faded, as her brain had interpreted that statement in a certain way, and she looked up at him, taken aback.

Noah blinked, realizing what she was thinking. "No, no." He waved his hand, straightening up. "I just meant we were always being chased by someone and running for our lives."

"Oh! Oh." She nodded. "Okay."

But the stray thought must have lingered in Laney's brain, and Noah caught her gaze dropping down to his mouth.

He looked away, summoning back his nonchalant façade as he definitely needed to clear something up. "Listen...I meant to apologize," he started, with a slight wince. "About— that kiss yesterday." He started to shake his head to explain. "That was—"

But Laney was already nodding. "It's fine," she said. "I figured it out already."

He shot her a questioning look.

"You miss Eleanor," she replied.

He stopped. "Yes," he answered and shook his head again.

"But I just wanted to make sure that you understand, it won't happen again," he stated firmly.

Laney huffed under her breath, almost in ridicule. "Sure, why would it?"

Noah narrowed his eyes. "Exactly. I mean, you have a boyfriend."

"Yes, that's right."

"Good." He nodded, letting out a little breath of relief before looking back out the window. "Then that's settled."

"Yes." Laney agreed. "We can be friends," she suggested with a tone of finality. She paused, furrowing her eyebrows. "Or friends *again*," she amended, looking thoughtful. "I suppose we already were friends," she inferred. "Right? I mean, you mentioned you've saved my life before."

He gave her a brief pointed glance. "A lot."

Laney frowned. He was making it sound like she was ungrateful, but how was she supposed to be grateful for something that she didn't even remember happened? "But you said I also saved *you* before," she recalled, pointedly.

He was more hesitant to reply, but after a moment, he finally said, "Yes."

She waited for him to meet her gaze again, before raising her eyebrows in a prompt, "And?"

And Noah held her gaze. It was another long while before he spoke again. "And...it changed everything."

Laney swallowed at the gravel in his tone and she couldn't look away from his intense blue eyes.

She did feel it. That strange feeling that somehow she knew him. But *more* than that, more than having known him possibly eight months ago, she felt as though she had known him all her life.

As though with just one glance, he was saying more to her than anyone else in her life ever had, saying everything that was unsaid, everything that needed no words to say.

Something she already knew, had always known...

Her heartbeat started to quicken its pace in her chest and it occurred to her why despite the obvious circumstances and plain logical facts, Noah had to be very clear about that kiss from yesterday never happening again.

Because it very well actually—*easily*—could.

A sudden ringing made Laney jump and she looked down at the robot on the windowsill.

The little robot beeped twice before a holographic screen flickered over its head.

"Berry!" Laney blinked in recognition of the face that appeared on the screen.

It looked like Berry was still in his office, back at GNR. "Hey guys," he greeted. "Just checking in, making sure neither of you've killed the other one yet."

Noah had stepped back, his arms crossed over his chest again. "She hasn't had that 'bleed through' again," he responded.

Berry smirked on the screen. "Yeah, that's not what I meant."

That made Laney laugh, any unease she may have had instantly leaving her. *Good old Berry.*

"You must have just left Singapore, huh?" he asked.

"Yeah, we should be in Wellington in the morning," Noah relayed.

"Any updates yet? On my cure?" Laney wanted to know.

Berry wrinkled his nose. "Sorry, I've only just started again. It could be a few days before I know anything conclusively."

"A few days?" she moaned. "I'm sorry, just how many days did you figure I would be stuck here anyway?"

"I'm really sorry, Laney," Berry said, shaking his head. "It's hard to say, but we're all doing the best we can."

Laney sighed. "I know, sorry. I suppose it's not your fault," she conceded.

"I've arranged for someone to meet you as you come off the ship," Berry told them. "To escort you to Dr. Chambers' lab. Don't worry, Laney. I promise you, we're going to sort this all out."

"Thanks, man." Laney smiled.

"Hey Noah," Berry called out. "I saw some kind of spike on Laney's CCL a while ago. Did something happen?"

"It wasn't a big deal," Noah dismissed. "She channeled a 'bleed through', but it was non-combative."

"Apparently, it seems in some alternate worlds, I was Japanese or something," Laney put in, before adding. "If only all the 'bleed throughs' were useful like that, instead of ones who're trying to murder people."

Berry shrugged. "I'm afraid at this point, we can't pick and choose which versions of you come through. But perhaps we can try to determine a pattern with them and see why you're manifesting these particular ones. I'll know more once I have more data."

"More data?" Laney repeated, displeased as it meant more 'bleed throughs'. "How about finding a way to suppress them altogether?" she suggested. "Then maybe my nanny here," she said, gesturing to Noah. "Won't be so protective—of *others*," she added wryly.

Noah shook his head but didn't respond to her baiting.

Berry grinned, but he looked thoughtful as he considered her suggestion. "Well, we'll see how it goes. Alright guys," he bade. "Just hang tight. I'll check back in once you've arrived in Wellington. Over and out."

***

"What are you doing?" Noah leaned over, looking over her shoulder.

Laney turned sideways. "Oh," she said, gesturing to P.T. perched by the windowsill next to her seat, a holographic screen above its head displaying flickering videos of something in black-and-white. "I was bored and I found these on P.T."

Noah looked taken aback. "P.T. can play 'I Love Lucy' clips?"

"I guess so," she said. "Didn't you know that?"

He was still looking at her strangely. "How did you even get that to work?"

Laney shrugged. "I don't know," she said. "Berry said it's had some upgrades. I mean, I just pressed this button, the screen came up with options, whatever." Then she shook her head briskly, gesturing to the show. "You know, I get that she's funny," she remarked offhand. "But some of this over-acting just goes over my head—" She stopped short as he was still staring at her. "What?" she prompted, before rationalizing.

"I've been sitting here for hours. There wasn't anything else to do—"

He dismissed it. "It's fine. It's just sometimes I forget that you are also Laney—I mean, Eleanor. Berry *did* say you were a fast learner."

Laney broke a smile, looking pleased. Then she glanced out the windows briefly to watch the clouds sail past, before remembering something she had wanted to ask, since, in Laney's entire life, the farthest she had ever gone away from home was Disney World. "Hey Noah," she started. "This place where we're going—Wellington? What's it like?"

Noah settled back in his seat. "Windy."

"That's it?"

"I'm not a tour guide," he said flatly.

She smirked and elbowed him, teasing. "Come on, yes, you are."

"Why don't you ask your little robot friend, it's just had an upgrade, surely it must have all this information."

P.T. had tipped onto one side and was trying unsuccessfully to roll over, his wheels screeching in effort.

Laney glanced over and set it upright on the windowsill again. "You know I don't speak robot."

"I'm not so sure about that," Noah mumbled, huffing to himself, before giving her a look. "Look, this is not a tour. You're not on vacation here," he pointed out. "We're on a very important mission. You need to stay focused."

She shook her head again. "Boy, you really know how to suck the fun out of stuff."

And Noah just narrowed his eyes at her again. "Are you always this annoying when no one's trying to kill you?"

Laney stuck her tongue out at him.

Just then, the little signs mounted on the cabin ceiling clicked again, switching from saying 'COMMUTER AIR' to 'DEPRESSURIZED', and Noah looked up. "We're almost there."

Laney's eyes lit up. "Hey, that means I can go outside and have a look." She stood up, glancing back at him, still leaned back against his chair. She raised her eyebrows in a prompt. "Come on."

"I've seen it before," he replied, not moving.

She tilted her head slightly and held out her hand. "Then show *me*."

8

Coming Home

The airship was flying silently over rolling green hills, dotted with about a million sheep, paved little laneways tracing a winding route around the greenery, with quaint clumps of bungalow houses covering the hillsides.

In the distance, several dozen wind turbines mounted on hills were spinning to provide renewable energy to the smallest capital of the world. On the horizon rose a busy metropolis, providing a stark contrast to the peaceful countryside. There were also a couple of other smaller airships aloft in the area.

Laney smiled in wonder as she looked out over the deck railing.

Noah was watching her face, standing beside her. "What is it?"

"I don't know," she replied. "It feels..." She shook her head at the view. "It's so beautiful. It feels like—"

"Like what?"

"Like home."

P.T. chirped twice.

Laney smiled again. "Yup."

The airship flew over a row of artsy wind sculptures situated along the waterfront, then a fountain in the middle of a bay, shooting water up, across from a beachside area that looked to be packed with people.

Laney looked ahead, spotting the marina where the airship was going to make berth, and she saw that there were other old boats docked along a walkway lined with colorful streamers.

"What's that?" She squinted as she could faintly see something under the water further along the harbor, something else that was docked at the marina—or it *was* docked, and was at the moment just pulling away, sending ripples of water crashing against the buffers before it submerged deeper into the water, disappearing from view completely. "Whoa, was that a submarine?"

Noah glanced over. "Yeah." He nodded. "That's the mobile submersible lab. Berry's had some repair crews working on it, making a few upgrades here and there. It's way better now than last time you were in there—" He rapped on the railing twice in despondence. "That you don't remember, of course." He blew out a breath in slight frustration.

She frowned. "I feel like I should be sorry for not remembering any of this."

"No, *I'm* sorry." He shook his head. "Maybe...it would have been better if we didn't try to make you forget in the first place." He sighed again. "Well, there's no telling what would have happened, and in any case, it's too late now."

Laney's stomach felt like it nosedived when the airship swung sharply down.

Noah caught her arm to keep her steady. He was already looking up at the airship's large envelope being whipped with the sudden rise in the wind, and he bit back a small smile. "And now, we're definitely in Wellington."

There were a lot of people waiting at the arrival area where the airship docked. It seemed some of the scientists stationed outside of The Community rarely visited home—Noah included, so there were a lot of eager faces greeting everyone coming off the ship.

Laney amused herself to think that it must have been what coming off the Titanic would have looked like. She followed Noah down the ramp leading off the ship, and a familiar face was standing at the end of the walkway.

"*Kia Ora*, folks!" he greeted Noah and Laney with a small salute as they came down. "Welcome to New Zealand!"

"Hi, Berry!" Laney smiled in reply before she stopped way short. "Wait—what?"

"Hi Miss Carter, Dr. Donovan." Berry nodded at each of them.

Same wheat blond hair, same glasses. Except, he was wearing a proper suit and tie.

Laney frowned, confused, as she walked up to him. "I thought you had to stay at GNR to do all those tests and stuff?"

"Oh." Berry jumped as though he realized something. "Sorry. This is Berry's AI prototype. It's designed to simulate an exact replica of Dr. Berry Vermillion."

Noah's eyes widened. "Cripe, I'd almost forgotten what Berry's last name was."

Laney's eyes were also wide as she warily peered closer at him—it. "No kidding." She breathed. "Whoa...he looks so real." She had to squint *really* hard in order to even detect the faint mechanical joints. "I guess Berry had to level up from building tiny robots eventually, huh?" She cast a glance down at P.T. in her pocket. "What do you think, P.T.? You've got a big brother of sorts."

"It utilizes the cutting edge of meta-materials science to simulate human skin tone and elasticity," the Berry-AI went on. "As well as voice approximation and a complete faculty for physical movements. It is also designed to have a grasp of humor, and as a bonus add-on feature, it can be configured to converse using a wide variety of contemporary slang. What up, bruh?" He chucked his chin up with a grin. "Would you like to enable this feature—?"

"NO," Noah cut in almost immediately.

"Dude, it's going to be really creepy if you're going to keep referring to yourself in the third person as 'it'," Laney remarked.

"Noted," Berry-AI replied with another nod. "*I* act as Dr. Vermillion's liaison on this side of the world. *I* was only activated at oh-six-thirty hours this morning, so *I'm* still running in alpha-testing mode, but *I* am, of course, a learning program. *I* have been tasked to receive you on this end of the world to accompany you to Dr. Chambers' lab." Then Berry-AI gestured to his right. "This way please."

"Whatever, I'm still reeling from remembering Berry's last name," Noah muttered under his breath, even as he moved to lead the way.

And Laney laughed.

As they walked past the port docks and onto the boardwalk to head further into town, Laney couldn't help looking around in absolute and complete wonderment.

The weather was stunning and everyone was out—everyone, that was, what looked like the entire population of about a dozen high schools, as there were barely any adults around. "Jeez, it's like 'Lord of the Flies'," she mumbled in amusement.

"Interesting analogy," Berry-AI remarked, glancing over at her. "Have you read the book?"

She raised her eyebrows. "I read the Cliff's Notes."

"You mean the Coles Notes?" Noah prompted.

"What?" Laney asked, looking at him as though she'd heard wrong.

"Interesting," Berry-AI remarked again before addressing Noah. "In our dimension, Coles Notes was never adapted for other countries. On the other hand, Coles Notes was revised to bear the name Cliff's Notes, named for Clifton Hillegass, an acquaintance of Jack Cole, after the 1950s in *this* Laney's world."

Laney shot Berry-AI a strange look. "How do you know what went on in *this* Laney's world?" she asked, pointing to herself.

"Aside from a huge database of information, *I* am also equipped with all the data gathered from the *Quantum Jump*

Project, including the records regarding the worlds that were surveyed during the project," Berry-AI relayed.

"I thought everything related to the program was destroyed during the military siege of the lab?" Noah asked, looking displeased.

"A team has been trying to reconstruct what was lost from archives and offsite backups. This work has been ongoing since the military seceded from GNR. *I* have partial records recovered, but they are not 100% complete as of today."

Noah cursed sharply. "That damn Berry," he muttered, looking livid.

Laney shot him a look. "What's the matter?"

"He didn't tell me." Noah gritted his teeth. "He knew I would be totally pissed off so he didn't tell me."

"What's wrong with recovering a bunch of records?" she asked, confused.

"*I* believe Dr. Donovan is upset because the destruction of all the records was one of Dr. Laney Carter's last wishes," Berry-AI inferred.

And Noah glared at him.

"*I* believe Dr. Donovan doesn't like it when someone else spells out what he's feeling," Laney whispered loudly to Berry-AI.

Berry-AI blinked at her. "Noted."

She met Noah's still-dark gaze briefly in amusement before she shook her head.

Noah cleared his throat as though prompting them to change the subject. "Dr. Chambers' lab is at the University," he said, pointing to the furthest clump of buildings on top of a hill, seemingly across town. "There."

Laney's gaze traveled up the hill toward where he pointed. "Are we just walking?" she asked, surprised.

"This is Wellington," was Noah's matter-of-fact reply. "Everyone walks."

They passed a beautiful old red brick building with a clock face above a set of columns.

Laney craned her neck to look through one of several revolving doorways and from across the wide lobby, she could just see the smoke from a black steam engine train wafting over the train tracks behind the building. "Wow..." she marveled.

Everything looked almost normal enough to Laney that she could almost think she was back in her own world, except for the few details here and there that were distinctly other-worldly.

There weren't many tall buildings and most of the architecture looked like a fusion of well-preserved colonial English and modern Asian techno. Instead of neon, holographic signs flickered above shops.

It was absolutely mind-boggling to think that this small country now consisted of every other nation in the world.

Laney's eyes were drawn up toward a large holographic billboard mounted on what looked like the 'Good Year' blimp as its screen switched on just then, and a curly-haired boy of about twelve years old appeared on it.

"Good morning, citizens! In these trying times, I'm calling on each and every one of us to always choose hope. Hope in the face of uncertainty. In the face of difficulty. The belief that there are better days ahead. The audacity of hope."

"That's President Lineham," Berry-AI relayed.

Laney nodded *oh-really*, listening intently, as the President went on.

"Ask not what your Community can do for you, but what you can do for your Community. Be well!"

"Wow," Laney remarked.

"And don't forget powwow on DFS tonight at 9:30! Oh, and to that guy who crashed my flight sim server last night—huttboi five-oh-one-oh—whoever you are, be careful I don't confiscate all your F-18 jet model skins."

And Laney couldn't help a laugh. "Wow."

"He's...smarter than he looks," Berry-AI said, looking almost apologetic.

"I hope so," Laney said, still chuckling.

"As a matter of fact," Berry-AI began. "President Lineham has a Ph.D. in Anthropology. He co-wrote a paper on 'Global political strategies for multi-faceted small-scale governing synergy'. He won a Nobel Peace Prize. We're actually lucky he ran for president. Not many intellectuals have the stomach for the big office."

"Really?" Noah raised his eyebrows. "I thought he ran for president just so he could get to host country-wide MMORPG gaming tournaments."

Laney laughed again. "I'm not sure a twelve-year-old president is something I'm going to get used to any time soon."

"Where are you going?" Noah asked as Laney veered off to the left.

"Uh, the University?"

Noah jerked his thumb to the right. "It's this way."

Laney shot him a look. "Right, of course." She nodded. "I

don't know why I thought there was a shortcut through this street," she mumbled.

Berry-AI glanced up. "Actually," he began, meeting Noah's gaze. "There is." He gave Laney a questioning look. "But being that you have never been here before, it would have been improbable for you to have known that."

Laney met Noah's gaze briefly again but she just shrugged. "This does sort of look...familiar somehow."

Berry-AI tilted his head before suggesting, "New Zealand was largely unaffected by the cascade bomb fallout, so a lot of the things here are as they have always been. Perhaps this country has even developed in the same way as the one in your world."

Laney raised her eyebrows, casting the street a cursory once-over look.

The three of them had stopped to cross the street, waiting for the light to change on an air drone directing traffic in place of a traffic signal.

The girl in front of Laney, wearing a stylized bowler hat with an all-black floor-length taffeta dress, was talking on a hologram-type phone on a chain around her wrist. She moved aside to let a guy walk his bicycle past. Then the guy paused, pressed a button on his road bicycle, making it shrink down to about three inches big, stuffed it into the pocket of his moleskin trousers, and kept walking.

And Laney wrinkled her nose. "Somehow, I doubt it."

9

Tremors

Laney felt the cool air rush past her face as the three of them turned down a shaded alley and she looked up ahead.

A large dimly lit tunnel was sheltered between the pastel-colored buildings. Laney thought it was an odd place for a tunnel, but it seemed to be in no way obscure as quite a few other people were headed toward it as well. Then she saw it—the trolley car painted cherry red, with pale shuttered windows and a shiny number plate, waiting at the station.

"Is that a cable car?" Laney looked surprised.

"Technically," Berry-AI spoke up. "This is a *funicular* cable car since the car is attached to the rail, but this is the oldest functioning funicular cable car in the world." He went on, "Although, I do believe that there is still another one in Norway that *is* still functional, but for obvious reasons, it is no longer used."

Noah met her gaze. "We need to take the cable car to get up to the University," he explained.

"Oh." She nodded, before narrowing her eyes. "I thought you said 'everyone walks' in Wellington?" she mocked his earlier statement.

"Up a hill? Don't be ridiculous."

"The funicular goes up an incline of about 18% through three tunnels and three bridges, rising 120 meters—that's 394 feet up the hill," Berry-AI went on as he and Laney followed Noah and nearly a dozen other people who were in line to board the cable car.

Laney paused, furrowing her eyebrows as she strained to hear the music playing in the tinny radio mounted up front beside the driver's seat. "What is this music—is that *Crowded House*?" she asked, as she settled into a bench seat.

"Of course." Berry-AI nodded with a smile.

"This same song was also playing at docks...and the airship," she noted in recall.

"It plays everywhere," Noah said, offhand.

"Crowded House is the most famous band in our world," Berry-AI relayed. "Are they on yours too?" he asked, before relaying. "My records regarding your world's music cut off at around about the 1970s."

She made a face, somehow not wanting to ruin his enthusiasm for the 'most famous band' claim, and replied as diplomatically as she could. "Um, I've *heard* of them."

The cable car jolted slightly as it began to ease up the rail and into the first tunnel, creaking as it went on.

Laney turned to look out the window, eager for the car to emerge out of the darkness. This may not be a vacation, she thought, but she might as well enjoy the sights while she could.

Slowly, the cable car passed through the tunnels, and Laney could see the view from up the hill in the window. "Wow." Everything looked so green and so beautiful. She smiled to herself. She could still see the lighter airships aloft in the air across the sparkling blue harbor.

She glanced down in her pocket. "What do you think, Toto?" she whispered to P.T. in jest.

P.T. whirred in response.

She squinted upon spotting a large clearing in the distance, where there was a tall, narrow structure with a curled sculpture top, protruding amidst the rows of low buildings. It glinted where it caught the sunlight. "Hey, what's that?" she asked.

Berry-AI looked over from his stance, standing in the aisle. "It's a *Koru* Peace Memorial," he answered.

"Peace memorial?"

"It was built in 1953," Berry-AI began. "This country has always generally been peaceful, progressive, and through the decades, its culture has eventually been absorbed into everyone else's. Although the ease of achieving worldwide peace likely also stems from there being few enough people in the world that there are sufficient resources to sustain everyone, and therefore nothing left to fight about." He paused to conclude. "Consequently, there has been no war on this world since 1952, as that monument stands to signify."

"Wow. That...is absolutely amazing."

Noah's forehead was creased as he watched Laney's expression.

Not being of this world, it certainly sounded impressive to Laney. But she supposed Noah knew the worldwide peace was not all that it seemed to be on the surface.

She was watching the third tunnel lights change when she noticed that the lucky cat fastened to the front control panel of the trolley car had begun to rock gently up and down. She watched it curiously as the rocking began to get rougher. "What's...?"

But before she could turn to Noah to ask if he could feel that, the entire cable car jolted sharply up and down, as though someone had pulled a giant, invisible rug out from underneath it, and all the lights in the cable car and the tunnel flickered off, prompting some passengers to start screaming.

Laney's gasp caught in her throat.

Earthquake!

There was some loud rattling above the trolley, caused by big rocks falling down as the tunnel started to cave in. In another moment, a tremendous aftershock shook the ground, with the cable car giving a loud creak as it slowly began to tip over to one side.

"Whoa!" Laney cried out, trying to brace herself against the back of the seat, before she lost her grip and fell off balance, falling to the floor herself, along with several other people being thrown out of their seats, spilling onto the aisle.

Bags rolled off the overhead storage, brochures fell out of their dispensers, someone's push scooter crashed against a window across the way, cracking the shatterproof glass with a loud bang.

Then Laney glanced down toward the rear window in

dread as the cable car, having gone off its rails, began to slip off the steep incline. The cable car was going to slide down and crash into the depot on the street at the bottom of the hill!

"We're gonna crash! Look out!"

"Laney, are you okay?"

Laney glanced up at Noah in distress. "Am I okay? Do I look like I'm freaking okay?" she demanded.

Noah paused, his eyebrow still raised in curiosity, holding onto the pole in the middle of the cable car aisle, as he stood looking down at her.

For some reason, Laney had scrambled down to press herself flat on the aisle floor.

She let out a breath, before she turned, looking around at the other passengers sitting calmly in their seats, if not just staring at her strangely, inside the perfectly-fine, normally-lit cable car rolling slowly up the rails on the hill.

Noah's eyes lit up in recognition at the same time that he heard his HUD beep softly since his left hand was in his pocket.

Laney quickly scrambled back up, dusting herself off, blinking a few more times to get her bearings. "Uh, nothing," she said, her cheeks flaming red as she took her seat again. "Uh, sorry—sorry!" she apologized out loud, looking sheepishly at the people sitting behind her and across the aisle.

Fortunately, the cable car reached its destination at the top of the hill and Laney was glad to be on the move as she followed behind Noah and the rest of the passengers getting off. Her face still felt hot in embarrassment. She wanted to hide behind Noah for the rest of the day.

As soon as they were clear of the station and the crowd, and headed down the street again, Noah glanced back at her. "Do I even need to ask?"

Laney just pursed her lips and didn't say anything.

"Interesting," Berry-AI remarked. "Am *I* correct to assume that Miss Carter has just experienced a 'bleed through' in which she had a hallucination of a tragedy striking the cable car whilst we were on it?"

Noah replied, even as he kept walking, not looking back. "I think Miss Carter doesn't want to talk about it."

Laney let out a big sigh. "An earthquake, okay? I thought there was an earthquake."

Berry-AI's eyes lit up. "Ah! You might be interested to know that there is actually a big fault line that crosses the greater Wellington region. An actual recent significant earthquake had gutted several important buildings in town, such as what used to be the main library and town hall, as well as having done some major damage to the shoreline of the southern island. There has always been talk of the 'next big one' coming ever since the massive earthquake of 1855."

Laney stared at him. "No, Berry," she stated flatly. "I'm actually *not* interested to know that." She shook her head. "Jeez, it's like you want me to worry about natural disasters too, on top of everything else."

She glanced up at Noah. She was still frowning when she met his gaze.

His expression didn't change so that when he spoke under his breath, she almost didn't catch it.

"Are you okay?"

And Laney blinked, surprised at the timbre in his voice,

as it seemed to denote actual concern, but she just managed a resigned nod.

Berry-AI waved at them. "Dr. Vermillion is on the radio," he announced, holding his hand out for Laney to hand over P.T.

They stopped at the sidewalk and Berry-AI clicked a few buttons on the robot before the holographic screen with Berry's face came up.

"Just checking in, guys," Berry started. "I see you've met my AI prototype," he said with a big smile. It looked like Berry was in the 'airplane hangar' lab at GNR, while other lab coats scurried around busily behind him.

"Berry," Laney began eagerly. "He's amazing! I totally thought it was you coming to see us before."

"Yeah, thanks for the additional confusion," Noah quipped.

Berry shrugged, holding his palms out. "What? My face was the easiest pattern I could access," he explained. "Besides," he said, hooking something around his ear. It looked like an earpiece. "I'm also experimenting with a super-duper long-distance walkie-talkie-type thing with him too—check it out. Hi guys!" he greeted.

"Hi, guys!" Berry-AI said with a wave.

"You should try the milkshakes at *Sweet Mother's Café*—," Berry in the holographic screen started to say.

"They are phenomenal," Berry-AI said at almost the exact same time.

Then Berry grinned. "There's a bit of a lag, but—"

"There's a bit of a lag, but—," Berry-AI began.

"Oops!" Berry jumped, reaching up to click off his earpiece, and Berry-AI stopped transmitting, returning to his at-ease stance. "It's a work in progress," he explained. "But basically, you can talk to him pretty much as though you were talking to me."

At that, Berry-AI flashed Laney a giant toothy grin.

Laney cringed. "That's super freaky," she told Berry. "And he looks exactly like your clone."

Berry made a face. "Ewe." Then he laughed, raising his eyebrows in a prompt. "Do you get it? 'Ewe'?" he asked. But when Laney just shot him a look like he was crazy, he waved it away. "Never mind," he dismissed. "Cloning is so boring," he drawled. "If you ask me, the next logical step is human augmentation. In fact, some of our scientists are already working on replicating every organ in the human body in some manner of enhanced mechanical form or another."

"In the meantime," Noah interjected. "Maybe we can get a move on? We don't want to keep Dr. Chambers waiting."

Laney rolled her eyes. "Relax, the University's just around the corner."

Noah gave her another strange look, at her unexplainable familiarity with the area.

Berry chuckled. "Yeah Noah, relax," he told him, looking amused with himself. "You know, stress is linked to the six leading causes of death among the people in Laney's world."

At that, Noah glared at him. "And when exactly were you going to tell me about the recovery of the *Quantum Jump Project* data?" he prompted.

Berry's expression changed to guilty dread as his eyes lit up. "Oh! Oh no, sorry, look at that, uh, I think you're breaking up—," he announced. "The reception is getting really bad.

Noah, I'm going to have to hang up now. Sorry, guys. Talk to you later! Bye!"

And the hologram switched off.

Laney laughed and Noah shook his head.

Berry-AI quirked an eyebrow. "That was odd. *I* wasn't detecting any interference. The reception was perfectly crystal clear," he noted.

And Laney laughed again.

The main University building itself was beautiful, with gothic spires, stained-glass windows, and green ivy crawling up the external brick red walls.

Laney looked around the grassy courtyard leading up to it in awe.

Someone had planted different-colored flowers over one area of the lawn, with the flowers arranged to form certain shapes. She grinned as she recognized a certain iconic round arcade game character pattern chasing ghost shape patterns made up of planted yellow and purple flowers against the background of the verdant grass.

It was absolutely fascinating, Laney noted, which facets of her world had managed to make it through to this dimension. It was as though they were...inevitable.

She smiled to herself at the thought, glancing down at P.T. in her pocket again. "When we get a second, have I got a game to teach you," she said.

Noah led the way up the front steps and into the building, and Laney noticed the handful of young people around them all bustling around purposefully, most of them wearing lab coats or suit coats over quaint casual clothing, and she figured they were all probably geniuses too.

Then she craned her neck to do a double-take as she recognized someone that they passed by in the hallway.

Noah noticed her awkward movement. "What is it?"

Laney pointed out a blonde guy, who was stopped in front of a bulletin board and was juggling a few thick textbooks in his arms. "Holy crap, that's Kevin," she said, surprised.

"Who's Kevin?" Berry-AI asked, craning his own neck to see for himself.

"My boyfriend," she replied, before pausing. "I mean, back in my world," she amended. "Is he a scientist here too?" she wanted to know, looking impressed.

"Dr. Whitfield is one of our best researchers. His primary fields are mathematical modeling, combinatorics, statistics, and computer science," Berry-AI relayed.

"He's a Math geek?" Noah asked, furrowing his eyebrows.

"Wow," Laney breathed, still staring at him. "He looks hot in a lab coat," she noted, cracking another smile. "Would you introduce me?"

Noah looked annoyed and put one hand on her shoulder firmly to steer her back around toward the other end of the hall. "Need I remind you of a certain 'time is of the essence' warning from Berry, and 'expedience' being the theme of this mission?"

"What—hey," Laney protested innocently. "I just wanted to say hi."

"We are not here so you can flirt with your little boyfriend," he reminded her, his tone clipped.

Laney was studying his face. "You sound jealous."

He huffed, making a face in ridicule. "Am not."

She shot a self-satisfied look back toward Berry-AI who just grinned in response, even as she started walking down the hall again. "Whatever, jealous," she quipped.

10

Traces

They arrived at one of the larger labs on the south side of the building and found Dr. Chambers, the world-leading scientist in the fields of genetics and neurology, and Laney noticed, impressed, that she also had a certain inscribed plaque hanging up on her wall.

"Hi, I'm Maia." Dr. Chambers held her hand out to shake Laney's as soon as she walked in. "You must be the *other* famous Laney Carter."

Laney stared at her as she shook her hand. "Hi..."

Dr. Maia Chambers had dark hair, twisted up into a high ponytail on top of her head, almond-shaped dark eyes buried in dark eyeliner, and a tattoo of what looked like a seashell on the curve of her neck, near her collarbone—a complete contrast to Darla Addleton's fair skin, red bob, and green eyes—but that's who Laney felt she was when she shook her hand. She *felt* like she was looking at her best friend.

Laney narrowed her eyes at her before pausing, snapping back to the present. "Sorry," she said. "I just had a weird feeling."

Maia raised her eyebrows. "Hey, in my lab, we welcome anything weird." She smiled, looking up past Laney. "Hey Noah, how's it going?" she greeted. "Hey Berry-bot, thanks for bringing them up here."

"*I* am Berry's AI prototype," Berry-AI began. "*I* am designed to simulate an exact replica of Dr. Berry Vermillion. *I* was only activated at oh-six-thirty hours this morning, so *I'm* still running in alpha-testing mode—"

"I know, dude. I activated you," Maia said, her eyebrows raised.

"*I* utilize the cutting edge of meta-materials science to simulate human skin tone and elasticity," Berry-AI went on. "As well as voice approximation and a complete faculty for physical movements. *I* am also designed to—"

"Shut up, Berry," Maia and Noah snapped at the same time.

Berry-AI stopped talking instantly.

Laney raised an eyebrow. "Wow," she remarked with a laugh. "I bet you guys would love it if that worked on the real Berry."

Maia gave her a sly look but didn't respond to that. Instead, she gave Laney a once-over. "Well," she started, blowing out a breath. "I see Berry didn't exactly follow my advice regarding that memory serum prototype. I never suggested that he should test it on an extra-dimensional person."

"It was an emergency," Noah explained. "And we were really confident that you already had a working anti-serum. At least, that's what your latest paper said."

She chuckled at his almost affront. "You're lucky I'm brilliant."

Laney blinked. "So, you *can* fix me?"

"Of course," she replied, the confidence in her tone almost sounding dismissive. "I am ecstatic though about the results. So, she really doesn't remember anything from her time here before?" she asked, turning to Noah.

"Zero."

"And how long would you say it took for her to respond to the serum?" Maia prompted Noah again, her eyes shining.

"It was almost instantaneous," Noah said. "She displayed an almost instant recovery of her bearings, and she showed no recognition of any immediate visual cues."

Laney raised her hand. "Uh, *she* is standing right here."

Maia chuckled again. "Sorry," she said. "It's just amazing when you see your baby project work so well on its first outing—especially with a highly unorthodox test subject."

"So," Laney prompted with a loud clap of her hands. "Why not let's bring out the anti-serum and wham-bam-thank-you-doctor, I can shoot off home, shall we?"

Maia pursed her lips, her eyes narrowing. "I'm not sure what Berry told you, but there is no 'anti-serum' *per se*." Then she gestured toward a cylindrical glass enclosure, standing in one corner of the lab. "There is however a *memory-doohickey reversal* chamber," she said, grinning. "I'm still working on the name."

"Oh."

Maia walked up toward the control panels beside the chamber, turning up switches and dials, flicking on several lights, and the mechanism began to hum steadily.

Then she looked back at Laney. "We just need to get you inside this chamber, press the 'Go' button, and see what happens," she relayed. "But before that, I need to do some baseline measurements, and test the process on a small sample of your DNA first, to make sure there are no immediate adverse side-effects."

Laney groaned. "Ugh, you talk like Berry," she said. "I hardly understand anything."

Maia chuckled. "Don't worry," she assured, despite the catch in her tone. "I would never intentionally compromise your safety just to further my scientific research. That would be completely unethical."

Noah cleared his throat loudly, shooting Maia a very pointed look, as that was a very blatant jab at Eleanor's work ethic.

But Maia just smirked, undaunted, before looking over to meet Laney's gaze again. "So, let us begin, shall we?" she prompted.

Laney looked at Noah and Maia in turn as the two of them were obviously trying to hide something, but she just let out a resigned sigh, knowing full well it was pointless to ask. She just wanted the entire procedure to be over and done with already.

Secrets were one thing, but she was beginning to find being around giant know-it-alls with arrogant, inflated egos to be quite tiresome.

"Noah, why don't you go take a break or something?" Maia suggested, not looking up from her instrument table as she prepared her little gadgets. "You've delivered Laney safely to her destination, into my very capable hands. Surely, you've earned it."

"I'm fine," Noah said, leaning against a bookshelf, his arms crossed over his chest.

She shot him a look. "Seriously dude, this is going to take a while," she told him. "I know you're a tough guy, but you can't just stand around there all day."

He met Laney's gaze, looking hesitant for a split second. Then he shrugged. "Fine, I guess I could go check out the Physics lab, say 'hi' to the old team. I haven't exactly been here in a while."

"We all started out of this University," Maia told Laney. "Then Noah and Laney moved on to bigger and better things over at GNR."

"And a fat lot of good that did," Noah mumbled under his breath as he turned to leave.

Berry-AI perked up. "I'll go with you. Dr. Vermillion has a running bet about dark matter stars with Dr. Destefano that he's been eager to rub his nose in..." His voice trailed off as the two of them walked out the doorway.

Laney watched the two guys leave, before she blew out a breath, moving to sit on a stool at the table where Maia was preparing her instruments. "Thanks for that," she said. "I think I may have had just about enough of that guy for the last few days."

"Who, Noah?" Maia's eyebrows rose, looking incredulous. "Really?"

Laney's mouth dropped open slightly. "I mean, I'm just glad to have someone else to talk to for a change," she amended, trying to sound neutral.

"Ohh yeah." She nodded. "I suppose talking isn't what Noah does best, is it?"

Laney huffed in agreement.

But then Maia added, "He's pretty hot though." She wiggled her eyebrows. "Nobody else can brood like Noah Donovan."

Laney looked doubtful. "I guess."

Maia shot her a knowing look.

"Alright, fine." She threw her hands up. "I realize that he's hot," she said. "But I already have a boyfriend, back in my world. Kevin Whitfield. In fact, I think I saw him in the halls." She jerked her thumb in the direction of the door.

"Oh, yeah, Kevin." Maia nodded again, in acknowledgment. "He does Math Science—statistics, modeling, projections, those sorts of things. He's also pretty handy with technology. And..." She paused to consider. "I suppose he's also pretty cute."

Laney grinned. "Thanks." Then her expression faded slightly as a wave of homesickness hit her from the thought. She frowned. "I miss him. My friends. My world," she said, her chest feeling heavy as she met Maia's gaze. "Any idea how long this cure thing is going to take?" she wanted to know.

Maia gave her a consoling look. "I'm afraid all this is bleeding edge—excuse the pun, but nothing like you has ever happened here before. We're all just trying to feel our way through all this." Then she nudged her shoulder, brightening up. "Not to worry though. You can be sure that the best minds in this world are already working to help you. You're actually pretty lucky," she told her. "The only other thing maybe that we could probably use right now is—ironically, the *real* Dr. Laney Carter." She tilted her head. "I bet *she* could figure the solution out of this incredibly tactile paper bag in two seconds."

"I was *hoping* it was going to just take two seconds. I seriously can't wait to get this all over with so I can go home," Laney commented, looking tired.

"You know," Maia began, regarding her with another look. "This world is pretty nice. I don't know what your world is like, but I'm sure there are worse dimensions than this. So, even if it doesn't work out, you could always consider staying here," she suggested.

Laney looked at her, taken aback. "What? I can't stay here."

Maia shrugged. "Why not? You can't go home," she reminded her. "And from what I understand from Berry, you can't really go anywhere. And at least, in this world, we understand what's going on with you, and we can help you through it."

Laney was already shaking her head. "Thanks for the silver lining, but I want to go home to *my* world. That's where I belong."

Maia tilted her head slightly. "Belong?" she echoed, almost in ridicule. "I reckon you can belong anywhere you want. *Make* a home instead of being assigned it. 'Home' is just a concept anyway. Home is where you find yourself. You make a home where you are."

Laney watched her with a strange look, but she didn't say anything.

"Alrighty," Maia started, rubbing her hands together. "Let's get this show on the road."

She gestured for Laney to take a seat on an examination chair, before she stretched to reach above a cupboard to switch something on, and instantly, the lab was filled with some heavy metal beats and rock guitar screeching music.

Laney cracked a small smirk as she watched Maia move around the lab and it hit her. The eyeliner. The tattoo.

Maia's eyes lit up. "Oh sorry, do you mind this music? I forget sometimes that not everyone is into alt-rock."

Laney shook her head, still looking amused. "At least it's not Crowded House again."

And Maia laughed. "Yeah."

Laney watched as Maia stepped to the beat of the music at the same time that she filled test tubes, fiddled with some control panels, peered into microscopes, and Laney smiled to herself.

Darla—ever the musical one—was also almost always dancing around to some song.

Laney recalled what Berry had said the other day, about alternate selves and permutations, and she felt that it was totally conceivable that perhaps Maia was indeed the Darla of this alternate world.

Laney just felt completely at ease and comfortable around her, as though she was just hanging out with her best friend.

Except in this world, her best friend had a Ph.D. in Neurobiology and Genetics.

"Is that D.J.?" Maia cast what Laney was holding a curious glance.

"Oh." Laney dropped her gaze down at P.T., which she had propped onto the lab table, so she could fiddle around with its interface. "No, its name is P.T."

"Ah. I can never get their names straight."

"What do the letters even stand for?"

"You'll have to ask Berry," she replied. "That guy's a little bit too eccentric."

Laney smirked, resisting the urge to point out the 'pot calling the kettle black' situation. "Hey Maia," she spoke up instead, giving Maia a curious look. "When did you know you wanted to be a scientist?"

Maia glanced over, looking thoughtful for a second. "I think I've always been interested in genetics. My parents were scientists too, and every year for Christmas until I was about six, I always got a chemistry set," she relayed. "I think my folks wanted to nurture my interest in science, make sure I chose the same specialty as them. Although, I do believe that humans are genetically predisposed to certain things, so I figure I was always going to be a scientist regardless."

"I guess I'm still in awe over how accomplished you all are in your work when I *know* you are all just the same age as me," she remarked, still looking bewildered.

She blinked at her. "Well, you already know, right? Everyone in our world carries a mutated genetic enzyme that causes our brain cells to develop more rapidly than they used to, that is, before the global cascade bomb event in 1952. I wrote a paper about it."

Laney nodded, with a catch in her smile. "Yes, Berry told me about your paper," she said. "Makes me wonder though," she began quickly before Maia decided to go off on a tangent and start quoting passages from her famous paper. "Is everyone on this world a scientist?" she asked. "Even the President is one. But I think Berry mentioned there was a military sector, so maybe the answer is 'no'?"

Maia pursed her lips. "Hmm." She paused. "I do know of several people in the military who still have PhDs themselves—Noah being one of them."

"Right." Laney nodded before she countered, "Well then, who does your plumbing? Who takes out the trash?"

P.T. chirped as if in response.

Maia nodded in its direction. "Anything menial has been delegated to robots or machines that have been invented to serve a specific purpose, which are maintained *by* scientists. Even the underground system for water, gas, waste, and stuff like that is maintained by our Biological Systems Engineers," she relayed. "The system itself is a biological model based on the human digestive system."

"Oh-kay then." Laney's eyes widened.

"Oh, you know who we should ask?" Maia's eyes lit up.

"Who?"

"Kevin," Maia piped up. "It's part of his job to analyze the census on the population of The Community. He probably has access to records about what percentage of the population holds what type of educational and employment background."

Laney shot her a look. "Seriously?"

"Absolutely!" She nodded. "These cultures will take a while to develop anyway. In the meantime, why don't we see about getting you a formal introduction with the infamous Dr. Whitfield, hey?"

Laney looked wary. "Noah made it seem like it would be

a bad idea for me to interact with too many people here, let alone my boyfriend."

Maia rolled her eyes dismissively. "He's just being overly cautious. Come on," she coaxed, meeting her gaze with a grin. "You know you want to."

And the mischievous glint in her eye was Darla Addleton all over, and Laney couldn't resist.

II

Golden Halo

Noah was walking back toward Dr. Chambers' lab when he stopped short upon seeing Laney and Maia talking to Dr. Whitfield in the common area, standing around a work-station table piled high with books.

Berry-AI was walking beside Noah and stopped as well, except Berry was doing his walkie-talkie thing from GNR and was actually transmitting himself. "Is that *the* Kevin?" he wanted to know.

Noah cast a discreet glance up to where Laney was leaning close to Kevin as they were looking over some thick volumes of census books together, in time to see her laugh at something he said, and something in his stomach tightened, but he didn't say anything.

Berry-AI narrowed his eyes at him. "What the hell is wrong with you? Are you seriously going to let him have her?"

"*Let* him?" he repeated. "What do I have to do with it?"

"Uh, everything?" Berry-AI replied pointedly. "She doesn't even realize what you are. It's the inescapable truth, man."

Noah grunted. "That's just a theory."

Berry-AI glanced over at him. "Look at your face, even you don't believe you."

Noah gave Berry-AI an even look. "She's in trouble," he rationalized. "She's displaced. This isn't even her world. The last thing she needs right now is any more pressure from something she doesn't even understand. Besides," he added, almost authoritatively. "She knows she can't be with *that* one."

"Well, she has nowhere else to go," Berry-AI quipped.

Noah pursed his lips. He was annoyed with Berry, but he was really more annoyed with himself. "You know I can't."

"Whatever, dude." Berry-AI just shrugged before Berry signed off.

***

Laney noticed Noah and Berry-AI walking back toward them, but actually, she was more focused on what Kevin was saying at the moment.

As far as scientists went, Kevin was the only one whose field made even the slightest bit of sense to Laney, since it was all about mostly everyday things—the rate of population growth since the 1950's mass immigration, statistical records on what kinds of species of animals thrived across the country, how often it's snowed in Wellington for the last six decades.

"Not often apparently," Kevin relayed as he skimmed past a page in a big book. "Which I suppose is fortunate, since the infrastructure here is really not built for snow, with everything being on the hills and all that."

"This all sounds really interesting," Laney commented with a smile, even as she extracted P.T. from being buried under a pile of old books.

Kevin smiled back, glancing up at her. "Really? A lot of people don't think so."

She met his gaze, still smiling.

It was again, odd. She knew he wasn't the exact same Kevin from her world. Kevin definitely was no math whiz, but in all other aspects, she felt as though he may as well have been her boyfriend.

The Kevin who always thought about others before himself, the Kevin who always made sure Laney made it to class on time, the Kevin who always made her feel very well cared for.

"I'm stoked by these numbers though," Maia spoke up as she held another census book close to her face. "I always knew we had a lot of sheep and cows and horses and stuff, but knowing definitively that all the snakes in the entire world were wiped out with the cascade bomb? I might suddenly take up hiking."

Laney grinned, nodding in approval, and looked over to meet her gaze. "I think I may learn to like this world after all, Maia." She glanced over at P.T. "What do you think, P.T.? Impromptu camping trip?"

"Hey, folks!" Berry-AI greeted everyone as he and Noah walked over to the group.

Kevin straightened up from the table. "Oh. Hey, Donovan," he greeted.

Noah looked at him. "Whitfield." He glanced down at Laney before he met Kevin's gaze again, but he didn't say anything.

Laney looked at everyone in turn as they all seemed to have been stunned into silence. She furrowed her eyebrows in a puzzled prompt. "What?"

At that, Maia's eyes lit up. "Hey," she began, almost too loudly. "I think I heard my centrifuges stop spinning. I guess we'd better get back to work. Hey Kev, thanks for the info," she bid with a nod, turning to leave.

"Any time." Kevin shrugged with a smile. "It was nice to meet you, other Laney." He raised his hand in a small wave. "If you're ever keen to examine any other statistics, you know where to find me."

Laney smiled back at him. "Thanks, Kevin."

"Hey, Berry-bot." Maia linked arms with Berry-AI, leading the way away from Kevin's table. "Did you know that only two percent of The Community's population do not hold any manner of Ph.D.? They're mostly soldiers and artists. I didn't even know that."

Laney put P.T. back in her pocket, meeting Noah's gaze tentatively as she walked past him to follow Maia and Berry-AI back to the lab.

"You can't tell him," was all Noah said since he knew she would understand exactly what he meant.

Laney paused in mid-stride before she kept going. "I didn't," she insisted as he fell into step beside her. She was a little irritated that he would assume she would be that care-less. "I wouldn't do that. Why would I? I'm still hedging on the chance that this is all just a dream and that I wake up in my bed tomorrow morning."

"We should all be so lucky," Noah quipped, with a tone that was not in any manner joking.

Laney started to shake her head, looking mystified again. "It's just so weird to be around these people. It's like I *know* them, but I actually don't...but I *do*," she insisted. "And I don't know how or why, as they look nothing at all alike, but I feel like Maia is my best friend, Darla," she added, looking thoughtful.

Noah met her gaze. "And you thought my name not being Jake was weird."

***

Laney fidgeted. She was nervous as heck. She had already stepped into the enclosed cylindrical chamber and was watching Maia work on the console right outside, with P.T. sitting on the lab table beside her.

To a certain degree, Laney was dreading what kinds of memories she might get back because, from the sound of it, whatever had happened the last time that she was there must have been *uber* intense.

But Maia gestured a thumbs up and gave her a wink. "Don't worry, Laney," she assured. "This shouldn't hurt one bit."

"Shouldn't?" Laney echoed. She wanted to imagine it was just one of those machines that you have to get into for a security scan at the airports, and not one that messes with your brain, one that might possibly give her a complete lobotomy. Her gaze moved to meet Noah's.

His eyes held hers, his eyebrows furrowed as usual, but if Laney didn't know any better, she would've thought he looked worried. Or impatient. He was probably eager to get on with the mission so that she could go back to her own world and out of his life.

"Ready?" Maia prompted.

Laney nodded. "Uh, y-yes."

Maia pushed a button and the chamber door slid closed, and as the machine started up, Laney heard another loud hum from within the chamber.

After a moment, a bright yellow glow began to form at her feet. She looked down and watched as a golden circle of light emerged from underneath her, surrounding her, as it began to slowly move up her body.

"The chamber is programmed to detect all traces of the memory serum. The way it works is that it scans your bio-chemistry to locate the serum markers, and tags them for dissolution," Maia was explaining to Noah as the machine worked. "Fortunately, when Berry and I developed the serum, he had already thought ahead to ensure that the substance could be tagged for a subsequent reversal process."

She went on. "We *had* planned on developing a 'serum'-type antidote, one that could be administered with a syringe to easily flush the memory serum out of your system, but with everything going on this past year, we just haven't had the time to collaborate again to refine the design."

"And yet somehow Berry managed to build an AI clone in the meantime?" Noah pointed out, jerking his thumb in the direction of Berry-AI standing in the corner.

Berry-AI's eyes lit up before he explained. "Actually, *I* was built last year. Dr. Vermillion was still perfecting some of *my* learning skills over the course of the year and *I* had been kept in storage until he decided that assisting you and Miss Carter provided a good opportunity for a field test."

Meanwhile, inside the chamber, Laney had been breathing heavily in apprehension the entire time—four whole minutes. But once the golden halo moved up past her head, it instantly dissipated, and the loud hum faded away.

Maia peered up at her from outside the chamber, her voice sounding muted to Laney from the inside. "How you feeling?" she asked.

Laney blinked a few times, looking around uncertainly. She took one huge deep breath, establishing that nothing indeed hurt, before nodding in reply. "I'm alright."

Maia pushed a button that opened the chamber door with a sliding hiss.

Noah stepped forward to take Laney's hand as she stepped out of the chamber. He was peering cautiously at her face.

"Do you remember anything?"

12

Special

Laney looked up at Noah, then after a moment, she replied, "No."

Maia stepped up toward Laney to do some basic checks, waving in front of her face, checking her pupil dilation, her temperature. "Nothing...rushing back to you yet?" she prompted, using her wristwatch to check Laney's pulse.

Laney frowned in concentration, trying to recall anything more about her time here eight months ago, but nothing was coming to her. She sighed in dejection. "What's going on?"

"Why doesn't it work?" Noah asked Maia.

Maia looked at a loss. "Unfortunately, as I've said, the memory-doohickey reversal chamber is not capable of working as instantaneously as the serum itself," she began.

"Although, I do recall Berry mentioning once that things always worked funny with the Laneys," she told Noah. "Maybe she just needs a little more time. Or it might simply be that we haven't gotten it all, and she needs another session inside the chamber. It's hard to say at this point." She met Laney's gaze. "I'm afraid in this case, you're our guinea pig."

She feigned a gag. "Thanks, I feel so special."

"The human brain is a funny thing. We still haven't really figured out how it all works," Maia admitted, looking sheepish.

Noah sighed heavily. "So there's nothing we can do but wait?"

"You know," Maia went on. "In basic neurology, a treatment suggestion that might help to get your memory back is for you to see or hear familiar things, things from the past," she suggested. Then she glanced over at Noah again. "Noah, maybe you can try to jog her memory by talking about what happened last time."

Noah shot her a wary look. "Like what?"

"Like Paris," Berry-AI suggested.

"I went to Paris last time?" Laney's eyes were wide in eagerness.

Noah rolled his eyes. "Yeah, and you drooled all over your ex-boyfriend."

Laney's jaw dropped. "I did not!" She turned to Berry-AI, her nose wrinkled. "Did I?"

Berry-AI only smirked in response.

P.T. beeped and whirred as if piling on.

"Oh god, maybe this is a little late in the game, but do I really need all these memories back?" Laney asked, making a face. "I mean, can't you just fix me right now, regardless of what I do and don't remember?" she asked, looking at Berry-AI and Maia in turn.

"Well, what we're attempting is already tricky enough as it is," Maia replied with an uneasy fidget. "It would go smoother if everything was the way it was and you were back to your normal self. But don't worry," she reassured again. "You're not going to forget any memories you've formed since. You'll simply retrieve the lost ones."

Laney knew Maia was probably right, but she felt incredibly disappointed and helpless. And she had a sinking feeling in her stomach as the 'best case scenario' in her mind dissolved completely.

She *wasn't* going to be back home any time soon, not tomorrow, maybe not even in a few days. She might be lucky if she would be back home *this week*.

"Let me run some more tests so we can figure out exactly what happened," Maia offered, giving her an apologetic look. "But it may take a few more hours for the results of the chem panels."

"A few hours?" Laney moaned, clutching at her stomach. "I'm starving. Any place we can get some food around here?"

"The University cafeteria is—," Noah began.

"—*repulsive*," Maia cut in, her eyes wide. "Why don't you take Laney to that café down the street and get some waffles?" she told Noah.

At that, Noah gave Maia a dull look, pausing, before he let out another resigned sigh. "Fine, let's go," he said, gesturing for Laney to come along.

"Waffles?" Laney repeated. "Isn't it like way past lunchtime?"

"So?" Maia looked puzzled. "You can have waffles any time."

All-day breakfast. Sure, why not? Laney thought.

Berry-AI stayed at Dr. Chambers' lab to assist with the next lot of tests, as well as to analyze some of the findings so far, in case it could help Berry with formulating Laney's cure back at GNR, while Laney and Noah walked down the street to look for some food.

"There're vending machines everywhere," Noah pointed out. "Can't you just pick out a granola bar or something?"

Laney stopped walking. "Oh my god, is that bacon?" She sniffed. "I smell bacon cooking. Oh my god, I'm super starving. I need to eat *real food!*" She gave Noah a pointed look. "I don't know what it was like for you at ninja camp, but a bottle of whey from a vending machine definitely does *not* an entire meal make."

Noah huffed. "Like I've told you before, I'm not a ninja. I'm a scientist."

Laney stared at his back, then she dropped a glance down at P.T. again in her pocket. "Sure, a scientist that looks like that. Science camps would be mobbed, huh?" she mumbled so Noah couldn't hear.

Turning the corner, they found the source of the bacon scent at a small street-side café. The quaint café had tables set up on the sidewalk underneath little green-striped umbrellas. And upon finding a table and sitting down, Laney gawked at the menu.

"I don't understand," she said, turning the cardboard menu over on its back and over again, looking for something. "Where are the prices?"

"The what?"

"How much are things so you know what to pay for them?"

Noah blinked at her. "They're free."

Laney's eyes popped out. "They're what?"

"Everything is free," Noah relayed, speaking to her as though she was a child.

"You guys don't pay for things? You don't use money, like at all?"

"The use of money was abolished sometime in mid-1950. If you notice, we don't exactly have any shortage of anything around here."

She shook her head in disbelief. "Okay, I'm sold. I love this world. Maybe I will stay here."

Noah shot her a weird look. "Sold?"

Laney dismissed it with a brief wave. "Maia was trying to convince me that there were worse things in the multiverse than being stuck in this dimension," she relayed. "I mean, obviously I couldn't possibly stay here, but I understand her point. And I mean, no snakes? All-day breakfast? Free food? World peace? Come on!" she exclaimed. "Who in their right mind would have trouble choosing which dimension to live in?"

Noah gave her a flat look. "In the meantime, do you think you could choose a meal so I can place an order sometime this week?"

Laney threw up her hands. "I don't know how to choose now. If everything is free, I want everything."

He mocked. "That is such a *your-world* thing to say."

She made a face. "Alright already." She glanced down at the menu. "Just get me a toasted English muffin, with bacon and eggs—crispy bacon, eggs over-easy—oh, and hold the ketchup."

"No ketchup? Alright, weirdo."

"Oh, and a cranberry juice, but if they don't have that, peach iced tea, but if they don't have that, then I'll just have water—still, not sparkling."

"Oh my god." He sighed. "Maybe you should order your own stuff."

But she simply stuck her chin up at him, not intimidated.

And while Noah went up to the counter to order the food, Laney looked around at the other café patrons, watching people walk past, and she couldn't help a smile to herself.

She watched as an air drone flew out of the door just then carrying a paper bag of food.

Food delivery by air drone. Nice, she thought, grinning to herself as she watched the drone fly up higher into the air. "Look, P.T.," she said, gesturing before the drone disappeared around the corner.

For whatever reason, Laney felt very comfortable hanging out at the café. It was another one of those things that felt eerily familiar. And she wondered if Eleanor had used to go there often and if that was a memory bleeding through right then.

Then her smile faded as she remembered a similar coffee shop that she and her friends frequented just outside campus, and thinking if she would ever be able to go there again, if the last time that she had been there with them was the last time...ever.

Noah came back with the food, instantly noticing the glum expression on Laney's face. "What's wrong?" he prompted, as he set down two small plates with toasted English muffins on them.

Laney looked up. "Uh, nothing." She dismissed the thought. It was just like Noah had said. She needed to focus on the mission as it was the only way she would ever be able to get back to her world. Expedience. Not distractions. "Thanks." She gave him a cursory smile as she started on the food.

He watched her uncertainly for a moment, then he must have concluded that she was okay, as he began to eat his food as well.

"Hey," she started again, sounding hesitant. "Can I ask you something—and you won't just like grunt and ignore me?"

He tilted his head, looking a bit wary, but otherwise attentive. "Let's see."

"Doesn't it feel weird?" Laney asked, with her eyebrows raised. "You've been to other parallel worlds—other worlds that are so different from this one. You have the knowledge that it didn't have to be this way, here, like this. That it can be and it is different elsewhere," she finished, looking intense.

Noah paused.

But it was a fair question. One he probably already knew the answer to since it had been at least a year since their team had made the initial breakthrough of discovering the other parallel worlds.

He met her gaze. "This world is my home," he said. "It's as simple as that. I wouldn't have it any other way."

"Home," Laney repeated softly, recalling Maia's insights about the concept. "I guess I consider home as being a place where my family is." She thought for a moment. "Maia and Berry mentioned that you all age faster in this world. Does that mean your parents are super-duper old by now? Do they still live around here?" she wanted to know.

Noah stiffened a little. "They would if they were still alive," he replied. "As a direct result of the genetic mutation, since our brain cells develop faster, they degrade faster too, which doesn't exactly bode well for the rest of the body."

Laney's mouth dropped open in alarm. "Oh, oh god, I'm so sorry!"

But he pursed his lips, unaffected.

Despite the obvious pain of losing your family early on, it was probably also something that people in this world were already accustomed to.

It still seemed grave from Laney's perspective. Her parents were both alive and well and would be for several more years to come.

"Are...your parents around much?" Noah asked.

She met his gaze, surprised at his question, but she nodded. She didn't want to dwell on the topic as it seemed cruel and unfair to him, but she realized that Noah would have had no idea what it was like to have grown-up parents.

"Sometimes more than I'd like," she said ruefully, before meeting his gaze again to add, almost sympathetically. "It's awesome."

A corner of his mouth turned up at how she had balanced her statement, but he just went back to eating his food.

Then he winced, hissing slightly as the salty seasoning on his food grazed the cut on his mouth, which hadn't yet healed from when Laney had phased and attacked him in Berry's office back at GNR.

Laney looked up, wincing as she realized what it was. "Oh,

I'm—so sorry about that too, by the way." She gestured to his cut. "If I hurt you."

Noah paused for a moment. "I've had worse," he told her. "And if I'm not mistaken, now that you're back, I have a feeling it's all downhill from here," he said with a smirk.

She laughed lightly, her shoulders shaking. And almost instinctively, she reached her hand out to touch the corner of his mouth with her fingers, and Noah drew back quickly.

She blinked. "Sorry." She dropped her hand, feeling like she just got drenched with a bucket of cold water.

Chill the heck out, Carter. You are absolutely not on a date, she scolded herself.

She cleared her throat, averting her gaze momentarily before looking back at him. "Um, we were supposed to be re-freshing my memory about what happened last time. I know you didn't want to talk about it."

But Noah's gaze had dropped to his HUD as he discreetly fiddled with it under the table and he didn't respond.

Laney stared at him. "Um, hello?" She waved a hand in his face.

"Hmm."

"Memories? Basic neurology? What Maia said? Paris?"

He didn't look up. "You'll remember it eventually anyway."

"And what if I don't?"

"Hmm."

Laney rolled her eyes. "I don't suppose you guys have a rule about no cellphones at the dinner table in this dimen-sion, huh?"

"What?" He finally looked up.

She gave him a pointed look. "Do you have to be doing all that right now?" she asked, looking exasperated.

"It's a message from the President," Noah explained. "I need to come in for a debriefing later today."

"Oh." Laney's jaw dropped again. "Whoa. Okay. Cool, a meeting with the President."

"And Maia needs us to come back to the lab to do some more tests, so she can recalibrate the test chamber before you can have another go later today," he said, hurrying up to eat his food. "So we'd better get back to the lab ASAP."

She nodded, even as she frowned. She was so not looking forward to that. She didn't want to keep getting her hopes up only to be disappointed again in the end. But as always, she knew she didn't really have a choice. The odds were just never in her favor.

But Noah was eyeing Laney's plate. "Are you going to eat your spiced tomato?"

13

The Alliance

"I thought you were a genius," Laney was saying in disbelief as she and Noah were walking back to the University after lunch. "We're talking about a *grilled* tomato—so no, technically, I don't think it's entirely cooked," she told him, gesturing with her hand.

Noah rolled his eyes. "What kind of person doesn't eat raw tomatoes anyway?"

"Hey, it's a legitimate condition! Some people just lack those certain taste receptors," she stated, sounding authoritative.

"Oh, some people lack those certain taste receptors," Noah echoed in mocking. "Look who's sounding like a scientist again."

She gave him an almost offended gaze but was unable to stifle her laughter. "What?"

Noah shook his head in mirth, recalling the last time

she tried to sound like a scientist, back in Paris. But before his mind could wander on that thought just then, he saw a shadow move from the corner of his eye.

His expression neutralized as he thought he glimpsed someone following them, but when he turned, all he could see was the several random people on the street.

Noah tugged on Laney's hand, turning the wrong way around a corner on purpose to draw out the person following them. "Laney," he started.

"What?"

"Don't panic, okay?"

She shot him an annoyed, instantly alarmed look. "How the hell am I supposed to respond to that?"

"Listen," he urged. "I think we're being followed. So what's going to happen is, as soon as we turn this corner, I'm going to start running. Do you think you can keep up with me?"

Her eyes were wide. "Is that really a question you want answered?"

In her pocket, P.T. chirped twice.

"Sshh, not now, P.T.," she hissed.

Noah kept walking as though nothing was wrong, waiting to reach the street corner. "I thought I felt someone watching us on the airship, but I thought it was nothing," he relayed in a low voice.

"And here I thought you said my life wasn't in danger this time around," she mused, even with the tinge of dread in her tone.

"I never said your life wasn't in danger," he corrected. "I *thought* nobody was trying to kill you. There's a difference."

"Okay, so now someone *is* trying to kill me too," Laney stated.

"I'm guessing that would be an affirmative," he acknowledged.

P.T. chirped twice again and Laney glanced down. "What?" she prompted, taking P.T. out of her pocket.

And just as they came up to the corner, P.T. burst a sudden puff of white smoke, which punctuated Noah's breaking into a run.

His eyes widened. "Was that a freaking smokescreen?"

Laney's eyes were wide too. "What the hell!" she exclaimed even as she tracked behind Noah, slipping P.T. back in her pocket. "Good job, P.T.!"

"Some upgrade," Noah remarked. "Tell me if it's hiding some type of getaway vehicle in there."

Laney grinned. "I guess we'll see." She was already breathless as she struggled to keep up with Noah's long strides. "This feels—familiar," she gasped after a moment, referring to the running.

Noah smirked. "I'll bet."

He glanced over his shoulder discreetly, but the agents following them had realized that they had been discovered, and they no longer made an effort to hide as they came trampling over the handful of people on the sidewalk, inciting several '*Hey*' and '*Watch where you're going*' as they pushed and shoved past.

Noah cursed sharply as one of them appeared a few feet away ahead to block their way. And when he glanced back, there were three coming at them from behind as well.

Noah leaped at the one blocking the way to quickly disarm

him, while Laney vaulted up over a bus bench *parkour*-style, before delivering a swift, spinning kick to one of the agents behind them.

Noah swatted the agent unconscious then he looked up. "Laney!"

He watched in bewilderment as she set off to attack three more agents all at once—effortlessly, before he fought past a few agents himself, running up toward her, and bracing himself with his back to hers.

"What do you think you're doing?" he asked, glancing sideways.

"Apparently, I'm doing your job, Donovan," she replied, pausing before she launched herself onto another agent coming toward her and easily subdued him.

Noah's eyes lit up in recognition.

Laney was "phased" again. This time to "Kickass Ninja" chick.

But Noah didn't have time to worry about that just then. And at least she wasn't trying to kill *him* for a change.

Agents were coming from everywhere, and at the moment, Laney was succeeding in clobbering them all, one by one.

Noah blinked, impressed. *Whoa.*

Laney felled another agent before she glanced back at Noah, raising her eyebrows in a prompt, "Well?"

He bit back another smirk as he followed suit behind her.

She was headed purposefully away from the open area, toward the top of a hilly landscaped garden, out of which another half-dozen agents were emerging.

Then Noah spotted Laney coming back to him.

"Heads up!" she called out.

As if instinctively, Noah reached his hand out for her and she anchored onto it, while the rest of her flew up sideways, tracking her feet up onto and across a wall, before landing a couple of effective kicks at two agents behind them.

Laney's feet landed on the ground and she met his gaze for a moment, her eyes shining with triumph before she pushed off again to run.

He grinned as he sprinted after her, running ahead, headed downhill into the lush green gardens.

The next path that Noah and Laney turned onto led to an empty grassy clearing—a dead end.

Noah stopped short, panting before he whirled around.

One moment, the clearing was empty. Then as though it happened in a split second, they were surrounded by easily three dozen agents—all teenagers—boys, girls, all dressed in long off-white trench coats with buttons all down the front, with the same slicked-back hairstyles, same shoes, same neutral facial expressions.

Noah held his arm back to shield Laney as he looked around cautiously.

But these agents didn't advance or seem to move otherwise. They all just stood in their stances, watching Noah and Laney silently.

"What's going on, Noah?" Laney asked, trying to even out her ragged breathing.

Noah straightened up, sensing that she had phased back to herself. "Just stay close to me," he said to her, under his breath. Then he called out loud. "Jacob! Come on, dude. I know you've got to be out there."

Almost out of nowhere, one guy stepped forward from

among the other agents crowding the grassy lawn, even as some of them were also perched against the surrounding hill above and around them.

Jacob had silver-white hair and was also wearing the same outfit as the others. But when he looked up at Noah, he smiled. "Dr. Noah Donovan," he greeted with a formal tone. "It's been a while."

Noah's face darkened. "So you're doing this out in the daylight now, in plain view of the public?"

"They don't see us," Jacob told him, looking confident. "We're just a momentary blur and then we're gone."

Noah huffed then he tilted his head slightly to remark. "I thought you and your little crew had disbanded completely after Blakely kicked it."

Laney made a face as she probably recognized the name from her world, but she definitely looked like she was busy trying to imagine that she was someplace else entirely.

Jacob simply bit back his grin. "You of all people should know better than that." Then he shook his head. "Don't think we've forgotten what you owe us."

"What is he talking about, Noah?" Laney whispered.

Jacob's eyes lit up. "Ah, Miss Carter," he said, regarding her with a look. "Welcome back. Or perhaps you're not so welcome after all."

Laney frowned. "What is that supposed to mean?"

Jacob grinned again. He glanced back at Noah. "Your girlfriend back there is trouble."

Noah replied through gritted teeth, "she's not my girlfriend—" almost at the same time that Laney interjected, making a face, "oh, I am *so* not his girlfriend."

But Jacob just smirked before his expression cleared. "You need to surrender her to us."

Noah shot him a contemptuous look, stepping back even closer to Laney. "Just try it," he warned, glancing up furtively at the other agents in case they began to descend on them, but the other agents surrounding them remained immobile.

Jacob laughed. "Come on, Donovan," he said. "We don't have to play this game. You say 'try it', we will, we'll win, you'll lose, you'll die." He shrugged, giving him a knowing look. "Besides, this matter is a little out of your league, and our authority supersedes the President's."

"Since when?" Noah prompted in mocking.

Jacob tilted his head, his gaze condescending. "The President's jurisdiction is only limited to this world. Our mission is the ultimate safety of the multiverse, in *every* dimension, in *every* world."

"You're starting to sound like Blakely," Noah huffed.

Jacob smirked again. "General Blakely was an idiot," he said. "He was a megalomaniac who would have destroyed us all had he been allowed to proceed with his plan. You actually did us a favor by erasing him."

"It was an accident," Noah said, as if in distaste.

Jacob raised an eyebrow.

"You erased someone?" Laney prompted with a scandalized hush from behind him.

Noah pursed his lips. "He was trying to kill you," he replied hoarsely.

"Ah...super."

Jacob waved his hand. "Either way, the approach of *my* organization is the complete opposite of his," he relayed. "We want absolutely nothing to do with the other parallel worlds. We believe each dimension should just be left to itself. *Her* presence," he said, gesturing to Laney. "Here in our world is an anomaly. One that needs to be corrected." He gave him a deadpan look. "Immediately."

Noah gave him a sneer. "Berry's already working on a cure."

Jacob raised his eyebrows. "It won't be soon enough," he said, something in his tone hinting as though he knew more than he was letting on.

But Noah just clenched his jaw, standing fast. "You are *not* taking her."

Jacob chuckled, shaking his head again. "You know as well as anyone, Donovan, that if we really wanted to take her, we would have her already," he told him. "This was just a...courtesy." He gestured with his hand. "A little check-up on you. We wanted to see where your loyalties were lying nowadays," he added to Noah.

Noah visibly clenched his jaw.

"Besides," Jacob added airily. "We've still got a few ducks to line up." He turned to meet Laney's gaze with another cold smile. "But rest assured, we'll be seeing you soon."

Laney swallowed, her nails practically digging into Noah's skin as she clutched his arm.

But in the next second, all the agents pretty much simply, subtly disappeared, as though fading into the bushes somehow.

Noah swallowed hard himself, slowly straightening up as Laney moved up from behind him, her grip loosening on his arm. He shook his head in displeasure.

"It's okay, P.T.," Laney whispered to her pocket. "They're

gone." She took a haggard deep breath. "Who the hell were those people?"

"*The Alliance*," Noah said. "They call themselves the 'Guardians of Science'."

"Guardians? Of *Science*?" She wrinkled her nose in disbelief. "What the hell is that?"

"Basically, it's a consortium of people—scientists, actually—who want to control what scientific discoveries are made," he explained. "Based on what they think is too dangerous for humanity. Like the atom bomb. They're supposed to be a secret society. Nobody is supposed to know they exist, or at least, nobody can confirm that they do. They work outside the system."

"Hah. Like the 'Men in Black'."

"The what?"

"Nothing."

"They say they formed after the global cascade bomb event, to try to prevent anything like it from ever happening again." Noah paused meaningfully. "They were really against the *Quantum Jump Project* right from the beginning, since they claimed it messes with the way things are, the way things were supposed to be. You know they say a little knowledge is a dangerous thing? Well, so is a lot," he stated.

"Is that why they're after me?"

Noah looked at her for a while before responding. "You heard him. You're not from this world. You're not supposed to be here."

"Well, duh!" Laney threw up her hands. "Isn't that what we're trying to fix now?"

"Yeah, except they don't like to wait," he said. "They

couldn't care less what happens to you. The Alliance will be happy as long as you were no longer in this world, one way or another. If they had their way, you'd probably have been shunted off to a different parallel world already. Or back to your own world to deal with your problem by yourself. Or..." he trailed off.

"Or?"

"Well," Noah started, his eyebrows raised. "It's a much easier solution to eliminate you altogether, thereby ridding every world of the anomaly."

Laney sucked her breath in. "Alrighty."

"Whatever the case, they don't want you to contaminate this world," Noah went on. "And the longer you stay here, the higher that possibility becomes likely."

"What the—am I like a ticking time bomb?"

He gave her a strange look. "If you like that phrase."

15

Powwow

Noah and Laney made their way back up to the University, taking the back way through another garden leading to a little courtyard.

Noah was still looking around furtively to make sure they weren't being followed, but it seemed Jacob had meant what he'd said about leaving them alone for the moment.

Of course, Noah knew, it also meant that he was being serious about coming back for Laney later on, so he didn't want to completely drop his guard.

When Noah looked over, Laney was no longer walking beside him, and he glanced back, his forehead creasing.

Laney had stalled in front of a statue. It was mounted beside a park bench, in the deserted little brick courtyard behind the University, and she was looking up at it curiously.

He walked up to her. "What are you doing?" he wanted to know.

"This place... It reminds me of something," she said, her voice soft. "I don't know what it is. I can't tell if it's my memories coming back or a 'bleed through' but...this location." She gestured where she was standing. "It's... For some reason, it brings images to my mind." Then she looked up to meet his gaze, looking mystified. "Of you."

He stopped, only then realizing where they were. He looked around the courtyard.

This was the place.

It used to be their favorite spot. The two of them would sit on the bench and read the latest abstract submissions while powering through lunch. They would analyze the latest empirical formulas, spitball ideas for resolving the next crisis points that may have come up in the project, and plan working weekends together.

So it was also the spot, last year, where Noah had proposed to Eleanor.

Noah watched Laney warily, half-dreading, half-wondering exactly what she was actually remembering.

But Laney was still staring at his face.

"What do you mean?" he asked, looking uncomfortable.

She tilted her head as if in a trance. "A few days ago, back in my world, I think I...had a dream about you," she spoke slowly. "You and..." She furrowed her eyebrows, trying to remember more before she finished her statement with, "sparks."

Noah blinked. *Sparks?* "Pardon?"

She looked as though she was trying to grasp the wispy fragments of a dream. "I don't know exactly. I just remember you were there and…we were surrounded by sparks…" She trailed off, confused. "What do you suppose that was?"

He swallowed. "It could be anything." He shrugged, despite the inkling of a memory nagging in the back of his mind.

"Huh." Laney held his gaze for another second before she turned back to look up at the statue again, still looking mystified.

Noah cleared his throat, eager to change the subject. "Come on, we'd better get back." He waved for her to follow him back to Dr. Chambers' lab.

"What the hell happened? Where were you guys?" Berry, transmitting through Berry-AI, asked as soon as Laney and Noah arrived at the door back at Dr. Chambers' lab. "Laney's CCL monitor was going totally bonkers over here."

Noah glanced up at Maia who was across the lab, talking to a lab assistant, before she went to focus on a read-out from a control panel, and he pulled Berry-AI aside so that Maia wouldn't hear the hushed conversation. "The Alliance found us and Laney phased," he told him.

Berry-AI motioned his arm to Noah. "Let me scan your HUD."

"Not here," Noah said, glancing up discreetly at Maia again.

"What's the matter?" Laney asked, noticing his hesitation, and glancing up over at Maia herself, but Maia had moved on to examining some specimen slides through an electron microscope.

Noah stuffed his hand in his pocket, stiffening slightly as

he glanced out the open door to the hallway as another lab tech walked past. "I can't show my HUD around The Community," Noah told Laney, looking hesitant to even be mentioning it at all. "It's...one of those 'Top Secret' prototypes," he relayed with a dismissive tone.

"Oh, okay." Laney nodded with a careless shrug.

"Hey, you're back!" Maia turned to smile as she noticed them just then. "How were the waffles?"

"Um." Laney met Noah's gaze before she turned back to Maia with a smile. "Actually, I smelled bacon and I just couldn't resist," she relayed, walking over to her across the lab.

She quirked her eyebrow. "Surely you could have had bacon *with* waffles."

Laney chuckled. "What is it with you and waffles?" she asked.

"What? They're delicious!" Maia replied, sounding almost defensive.

Laney laughed again, casting a discreet glance over at Noah and Berry-AI still by the door, still discussing something between themselves.

Noah had said that The Alliance was a secret society, so it wouldn't be far-fetched to think that Maia probably didn't know about them either, so Laney figured she shouldn't say anything. She just gave Maia another small smile. "Next time, we can get waffles, alright?"

Then Noah and Berry-AI walked over, having concluded their conversation.

"Berry had to go to a meeting, but he says he's going to send the results of his analysis as soon as he can," Noah announced, indicating that Berry had signed off from Berry-AI.

"How did it go?" he asked Maia. "Did you figure out why it didn't work?"

Maia bit her lip. "Not really," she said. "I'm still waiting on some chem panels. I think it's close though. I mean, I honestly thought it was supposed to work already. I'd have to go back to the board and re-check the formulas. I just need a little bit more time."

"Time." Noah's eyes lit up as he glanced up at the large baroque clock hanging on the wall. "Shit, I have to go meet with the President now," he said, then he looked over at Laney again.

"What?" she prompted.

"You can't come with me," he said, then frowned. "But I can't leave you here by yourself."

Maia raised her hand. "I can take her to the reception. And we can meet up with you after your meeting," she offered.

Noah met Maia's gaze uncertainly.

"Don't worry," Maia assured with a small wave. "She'll be perfectly safe with me—and Berry-bot." She gestured sideways toward Berry-AI.

Noah looked over at Laney again.

Laney raised her eyebrows. "I'll be fine," she told him, a little in disbelief. He didn't seem to trust anyone at all. "I'm sure Berry-bot would be happy to shift his role from talking encyclopedia to a bodyguard for just a few hours."

Berry-AI flashed him a grin and a thumbs-up sign.

"Alright," Noah said finally after a pause, then he looked over at Maia and Berry-AI in turn, as though in silent instruction before he finally turned to leave.

Maia shook her head once he was gone. "Jeez, it's like he's

worried you'll disappear into thin air all of a sudden if he doesn't keep his eye on you or something."

Laney just met Maia's gaze. Obviously, Maia was not aware that that was actually an entirely plausible scenario, but she didn't want to alarm her. Besides, they were going to *The President's* reception. Surely, there would be enough security there to ward off The Alliance.

"Hey Berry-bot, would you hold the fort for a second?" Maia told Berry-AI, gesturing around the lab. "Laney and I need to get ready."

Laney blinked at her. "What do you mean 'get ready'?"

Maia shot her a pointed, authoritative look. "Well, we can't show up at the President's reception just dressed like this now, can we?"

***

"That's a joke, right?" Laney prompted Maia, as she and Berry-AI walked with Laney down the street on the way to the Presidential reception that was being held at some place called—

"*The Beehive*? It's not really called that," Laney asked in ridicule.

"It's the government house," Maia replied.

Berry-AI began his discourse. "It's the Executive Wing of the Government Parliament buildings. The architecture is meant to mimic the shape of a traditional woven form of a beehive. That part of the complex was built in 1977 by—"

"Sshhh," Maia shushed him fast.

Laney snickered to herself. "It sounds like it's implying

that all the politicians are busy bees, flying around, buzzing all the time. I mean, do they even have a queen?”

“Actually, the Prime Minister is female,” Berry-AI supplied.

Laney looked confused. “Wait, I thought you had a President—that boy on the TV.”

“We have both,” Maia explained. “They’re sort of…co-presidents. It originated from the coalition government concept. It’s how the ‘checks and balances’ system works. This way, not any one person has all the power.”

“We’re coming up to The Beehive now,” Berry-AI spoke up.

Laney marveled as she looked up at the strange round dome on the building of the government house coming up behind the trees. It was indeed shaped somewhat like a real beehive. She shook her head. “Surely, it doesn’t look this weird in my world.”

“When I get my next data import from GNR on the *Quantum Jump Project*, I can confirm that for you,” Berry-AI offered with a smile.

“Thanks, Berry-bot.” Laney grinned as the three of them walked down the paved lane, flanked on each side with the rolling green grass, which led toward the building.

Laney noticed that there were also some other people headed toward the wide main front steps.

They were dressed in formal clothes, top hats, and black suits, the women wore funny, frilly hats and long dresses. She guessed they were all likely politicians or scientists too.

She was still boggled at the knowledge that they were still, of course, all only kids.

A pair of air drones flew toward the three of them, as they approached the courtyard, to escort them into the reception.

Laney glanced over at Maia and Berry-bot, feeling apprehensive, and was glad that Maia had lent her a different, more formal type of trench coat for the reception, similar to the one Maia herself was wearing.

Laney also felt a bit strange about having left P.T. at the lab. She felt like P.T. had been the one constant thing she'd always had with her on this trip so far, almost like a security blanket. But Maia had suggested that it would not be appropriate to bring the little robot to the President's reception.

Laney looked up at the sculpted coat of arms above the set of huge classical columns, lit up in bright lights, as she followed behind Maia coming up the steps, and the drones led them through the ornate wooden revolving doors leading inside the building, across the checked-tile floor lobby, and down the hallway to the banquet room.

Laney's breath caught in her throat as they arrived.

The banquet room was a semi-circle-shaped room, with tiered-light chandeliers hanging from the ceiling, brocade curtains, a large modern mural on the wall, and holographic mood lighting across the wooden floor panels. The room was bordered by ceiling-high windows, outside of which you could see the city, sparkling in the orange sunset light, and right down to the harbor.

There was already quite a crowd at the reception and when Laney looked up, a familiar face was by the doorway. "Hey," she said, looking surprised. "You're here too."

Kevin's eyes lit up as he smiled at her. "Hi Laney," he greeted, then glanced behind her at Maia and Berry-AI. "Hi, guys, what are you all doing here?"

"Noah said he needed to debrief the President over

something. Probably something about the last eight months," Laney explained.

"Oh." Kevin nodded. "Yeah, sure, of course."

Maia was already eyeing a plate of *hors d'oeuvres* coming around, propped on another air drone, while Berry-AI just stood looking around the banquet room as if taking in every detail of the place for a report or something.

Laney glanced at the two of them before she turned back to Kevin, tilting her head to one side. "Why are *you* here?"

"Oh, I'm here for the Powwow," Kevin replied. "I'm Tech Support."

"Seriously?"

"The President takes Game Nights very seriously," Kevin relayed. "He hosts it across the entire country, 'cause why not, right?" He shrugged. "But it's been a bit more problematic recently because there are a lot more intricacies involved in Flight Sim games. For a couple of years, we just used to have DND and DOTA. Then, President Lineham turned twelve and suddenly Flight Sims were the shit," he added with a grin.

Laney laughed.

"Well, I for one am glad he stopped hosting DOTA Game Nights," Maia spoke up. "I mean, how do you even get any work done when you're trying to work on your strategy, learning all the new heroes' skills, and making sure your wards keep killing it all night, right?"

Laney laughed again, shaking her head. It was so easy to forget sometimes that she was in a room full of accomplished scientists and geniuses and mathematicians and economists and politicians.

If anything, Laney thought, looking around in wonder, the

President's reception sort of felt like a prom—a Victorian-themed masked ball.

"The Powwow doesn't start until later," Kevin said before offering. "In the meantime, would you girls like something to drink?"

Laney raised her eyebrows in mocking. "What, *Yoohoo?* Milkshakes?"

Maia looked at her strangely. "What's a *Yoohoo?*"

But Berry-AI interjected before Laney could answer. "Actually, Wellington is the Craft Beer capital of the world. We manufacture every kind of beer imaginable. Light beer, dark beer, pale ales, brown ales, stouts, porters..."

Laney's mouth formed an 'o'. She supposed with a world full of kids, a 'drinking age' was probably something that had been thrown out the window earlier on.

Kevin studied her expression with narrowed eyes. "You know what, I'll get you something good," he said with another smile before he turned to walk away.

Maia elbowed Laney, grinning. "He's such a gentleman."

And Laney colored slightly. *Yup.* That was Kevin.

16

Masked

Kevin had brought them some fizzy cider, which Laney decided tasted pretty good before he was summoned away to troubleshoot something. And Maia had gone on to walk around and mingle with the crowd, dragging Laney and Berry-AI along.

Laney was well aware that she was supposed to be keeping her socializing down to a minimum, but Maia had different ideas.

"*Dasvidaniya*," Laney bid the guy wearing a top hat and a crisp blue tux who gave her a smile before he walked away.

Maia shot Laney an impressed look. "Wow, that was amazing," she remarked.

Laney had done it again and had managed to converse with the Russian representative for the U.N. entirely in Russian.

Admittedly, it didn't feel as creepy to do when she knew why she was able to do it. Although, she was hoping that that was the only 'bleed through' that would come out tonight. She didn't want to ruin a perfectly good party.

"Oh, look." Maia nudged her again, gesturing across the room. "There's the U.N. representative for Germany talking to her American counterpart."

Laney sipped her drink as she followed Maia's gaze toward the elegant, tall, blonde girl wearing a corseted dress, who was talking to another girl wearing a bohemian-style long dress and a carnation feathered hat over her wild frizzy hair. "Wow," she mumbled.

The two girls both seemed to glance up in Laney's direction before resuming their conversation.

Laney glanced across the room and spotted a guy wearing a kimono-style outfit and guessed he was the Japanese representative, and she paused at a thought. "So, do all the old countries each get a representative?"

Berry-AI spoke up. "Each former country whose population makes up a significant percentage of The Community has a representative in the government, as well as others who have largely retained their cultural identity. It was noted in a study by Dr. Mary Douglas that it was especially the particularly rigid cultures that have survived the cascade bomb event."

Laney smiled to herself. "Fascinating..."

"There goes the oldest guy in the world." Maia gestured across the room, toward the older gentleman standing by the refreshments table. "Dr. Rosenblatt," she relayed. "I'm actually amazed he's out this late."

Laney looked over. "He doesn't look any older than my dad," she noted, looking puzzled.

"Oh, I think he's like in his *thirties*," Maia said. "*Really* old.

I'm waiting for his lab space to open up, you know, later. It's absolutely amazing," she commented. "It's like twice the size of mine."

"Dr. Rosenblatt's laboratory space is *exactly* twice the size of Dr. Chambers' lab," Berry-AI put in.

"Yeah," Maia piped up. "But everyone knows he just got it on the grounds of seniority."

Laney's shoulders shook slightly in mirth, most especially at Maia's absolutely blasé attitude toward her possibly succeeding someone else's lab space, which would only ever happen for one terribly grim reason. "That's cold, Maia," she remarked.

"What?" Maia shrugged. "We all only have a few short years for our scientific contributions to matter. We have to ensure our time is utilized efficiently."

Laney shook her head. She was still continually amazed at the level of everyone's ambition and drive—and *arrogance*, but she figured given the circumstances of their world, it was to be expected.

"Hey." Maia nudged Laney again. "Look," she said, pointing across the room at another girl. "There goes Noah's ex-girlfriend."

Laney's eyes lit up. "Noah's what?" She looked over, spotting the delicate-looking, petite girl among another group of people, just as the girl averted her gaze away. The girl had straight black hair and beautiful, big eyes, framed by impossibly-long eyelashes. "Wow, she's really pretty."

"Sure," Maia huffed. "For a medical doctor."

"Dr. Li is a cardiac surgeon," Berry-AI relayed. "She attends the cardiac ward up at the Wellington hospital."

Laney made a face. "She's a doctor?" She felt her stomach turn over in a stark reminder that she really must be the dumbest girl on this planet.

Maia gave her a look. "Oh, don't worry," she dismissed. "They only went out for a few months. Noah totally likes you better, I can tell."

"You mean he likes the 'real' Dr. Laney Carter better—the genius one," Laney corrected.

Maia shook her head, a smirk on her lips. "Um, I most definitely did not mean *that*."

Laney shot her a look of ridicule. "Shut up."

"You know, Noah's a really great guy," Maia started, her voice lowered. "He might seem stand-offish at the beginning, but I think that's just all that military training. Back in our University days, he was always the first one to volunteer to teach the younger children, and he always did it with such enthusiasm and patience."

"He did?" Laney looked surprised.

"He's also incredibly loyal."

She recalled how Noah protected Eleanor's memory at every turn. "Yes, he is, isn't he?" She narrowed her eyes, looking around again. She met the gazes of another two girls across the way who were whispering together before they turned their backs to her.

Okay, that was weird. Laney frowned. "Hey Maia," she started. "I know I'm probably just imagining this, but I feel like...everyone's staring at me."

Maia looked around. "Oh. No, that's not your imagination," she said. "That's just all the girls. They're jealous."

"Jealous? Of *me*? Why?" she asked, in ridicule.

She shot her a look. "Everyone knows you're with Dr. Noah Donovan. He's like Number 2 in the Rock Stars of Physics Hall of Fame."

Berry-AI gestured with his hand. "Perhaps *I* can put it in a way that you might understand, Miss Carter. *I* believe it is similar to what you would call on your world 'dating the school quarterback'."

"But we're not dating!" Laney pointed out indignantly. "We're not even together, like at all."

"Obviously, that doesn't matter," Maia responded, her eyebrows raised.

"Pfft, well, that's just ridiculous." Laney rolled her eyes. "Rock Stars of Physics," she mumbled in mocking. "If he's Number 2, who's Number 1?" she wanted to know.

Maia grinned at her, looking amused already. "You are."

"What?"

"I mean, the other Laney—I mean, you know what I mean." Maia waved carelessly. "She's such a legend. Especially now," she said ruefully, shaking her head again. "It's like Marie Curie all over again. When your own work destroys you."

Laney shot her a look. "What do you mean?"

"Well, you know, Curie discovered radium and she died of radiation poisoning. *Ipso facto*, Laney discovered the quantum shear and—*ergo*."

Laney's eyes nearly popped out of her face. "She *what*?"

Maia clapped her hand over her mouth. "Oh shit, I forgot. You didn't remember yet."

Laney was frozen in shock. "Maia," she warned. "Did you just tell me that the other Laney got killed by a quantum shear?"

Maia wrinkled her nose. "Not necessarily," she said. "I mean, technically, she got sucked into the event horizon, dissolving all her atoms altogether, but you know." She shrugged with a forced smile. "Who cares about the details, really?"

Laney's jaw dropped. "She-she...dissolved?"

Maia gritted her teeth, making a grotesque face in guilt. "I'm so sorry—!"

A bell rang just then and Laney looked up toward the doorway to see a few people entering the room. She guessed it must have been the President and his delegation arriving at the reception.

Laney spotted Noah enter the room with them, and when he glanced over, he easily found her in the crowd and met her gaze. But the entire Presidential delegation was walking over toward Laney anyway.

Maia spotted them too, her eyes wide. "Oh, you know what?" She took Berry-AI's arm. "I think we'd better...go check out those mini-burgers on that drone over there."

Berry-AI tilted his head. "But *I* cannot consume food, Dr. Chambers."

"Just come on," Maia hissed, dragging Berry-AI away with her, and leaving Laney alone.

Laney straightened up apprehensively, trying to quickly compose herself from the incredible shock of Maia's revelation before she turned to face the twelve-year-old boy and his entourage walking up to her.

"Miss Carter." President Lineham's hand was already extended. "It's nice to finally meet you."

A girl who looked to be about Laney's age came up to stand beside the President and she put her hand out to shake hers next. "Hi Laney, I'm Prime Minister Maloney," she said with a smile.

"Wow," Laney breathed in amazement. "It's—it's an honor to meet you both," she said, shaking hands with them both.

She noted that in spite of their age, both the President and the Prime Minister seemed to exude a worldly, regal aura, and Laney did not doubt at all that they were in fact, the highest leaders of this world.

"We do extend our deepest and sincerest apologies for what happened when you were here last time," President Lineham began, his tone gracious.

Laney opened her mouth to respond.

Everything was falling into place—the reason why nobody would tell her what had happened last time, what had happened to the real Laney, why the President himself felt the need to deliver a personal apology.

It was no wonder everyone was so skittish about discussing what happened eight months ago. The real Laney had tragically *died*!

But Noah spoke up first. "We *are* still working on recovering her memories from that time, Mr. President."

"Oh, yeah, sure." He nodded in acknowledgment.

But then Prime Minister Maloney rolled her eyes. "I told you that Blakely was nothing but a troublemaker," she mumbled under her breath, dropping her regal façade for a moment.

President Lineham blew out a breath in exasperation as if he was already expecting her to comment on that. "Yes Janet, I realize now that was a mistake. But we can't all be perfect like my predecessor, old President Nichols, can we?"

Prime Minister Maloney sighed, exasperated. "Please Michael, don't get started on your guilt-fishing trip," she said. "President Nichols has been gone for two years. You can't keep bringing him up every time you need to ace an argument."

"Not if you're going to make me feel like I'll be in his shadow forever," President Lineham pointed out.

"Maybe if you didn't insist on imagining subtext everywhere and reading between the lines when there's absolutely nothing there. Sometimes what a person says is exactly just what they mean. This isn't Psych 101," Prime Minister said, her eyebrows raised.

It was like they were two siblings having at it.

Laney pursed her lips as she watched their back and forth, observing with amusement that there were still obviously some aspects of maturity a person really had to grow into, as it couldn't simply develop in spite of a genetic mutation.

"Whatever. The point is," President Lineham spoke up with authority. "We regret what happened and we are doing our utmost to ensure that nothing like it ever happens again. Our first concerns, of course, are the best interests of all the citizens in The Community," he stated, then he met Laney's gaze again as if satisfied with himself.

"Thank you, Mr. President, Prime Minister." Laney gave them a grateful nod. "I'll be sure to remember that when I get my memories back." She met Noah's gaze and he gave her a short nod of recognition.

"By the way…I was curious," she went on, turning back to the President and Prime Minister again. "Is it true that the people in The Community are not all aware of what happened at GNR eight months ago? I guess you're probably still just planning the public statement about the incident. Seems important."

Noah shot her a quick warning look.

President Lineham's eyebrows furrowed, and Prime Minister Maloney looked at her, surprised.

Laney looked at each of them. "I mean," she continued, almost casually. "You were, of course, planning to properly honor the scientists who lost their lives, right? Maybe the scientists doing work to put everything right deserve recognition as well?" She tilted her head, seeming almost offhand. "These just seem like they're also, as you said, in the best interest of The Community."

Noah's eyes were wide in caution but he didn't say anything.

But President Lineham narrowed his eyes and gave her an annoyed look. "Well, I'm not sure how that's any of your concern."

And Prime Minister Maloney smacked his arm.

President Lineham winced slightly, pausing for quite a while, before regarding Laney with a look significantly different from earlier. Then when he spoke again, his tone bore an abrupt, diplomatic, but still condescending, tone.

"I understand from the records that your world is quite different from this," he began smoothly. "So it will be easy for you to look around and not realize the intricacies involved in ensuring the smooth running of a world like ours. We must be sensitive enough to know the difference between what the public *needs* to know and what they *ought* to," he said. "We run a peaceful community and we prefer it to stay that way."

Prime Minister Maloney met her gaze. "Rest assured, Miss

Carter," she started, wearing her best serene smile. "We are, of course, looking into how best to properly handle the responsible dissemination of the necessary information, give credit where credit is due. But the last thing The Community needs right now is to think that this government is unable to propagate the peace that we have been privileged to enjoy for almost seventy years. You wouldn't want to send the population into a panic now, would you?"

Laney blinked, agreeing with a quick nod. "Of course not."

"This is our world," President Lineham spoke up again, his tone firm. "The only world we know. The *Quantum Jump Project*, revolutionary as it may have been, was a 'need to know' project for a reason. If The Community started questioning this reality, if they thought they had a choice—a *better* choice," he emphasized. "There would be anarchy," he stated.

Then he tilted his head slightly. "Can I trust that your stay with us, however brief, will in no way result in anarchy, Miss Carter?" he prompted, pointedly.

She swallowed, glancing up at each of the two beefcake bodyguards flanking the President as they stared down at her. "Of course, Mr. President." She nodded again.

Then the twelve-year-old boy turned on his heel and walked away, with his entourage following suit.

Prime Minister Maloney gave Laney a regal nod. "Enjoy the festivities," she said before walking away herself to greet the other guests at the reception.

Laney blew out a breath. "Boy, so much for world peace," she mumbled before looking up to meet Noah's irate gaze.

"And just what the hell did you think you were doing?" Noah hissed at her.

"I was just trying to do the right thing," Laney replied. "You knew exactly what I was talking about."

"You're already in enough hot water in this world," Noah reminded her, in annoyed disbelief. "Don't you know better than to antagonize the sitting government? Why can't you just lay low until Berry figures out how to send you back, so you can be someone else's problem? Don't you remember nobody wants you here?"

Laney let out a suffering groan. "How could I possibly forget when you keep bringing it up?" she retorted.

He narrowed his eyes at her. "Why are you suddenly lobbying for honoring the scientists who lost their lives anyway?"

Laney gave him an even look before she spoke again, her tone incredibly wry. "I just found out what happened to Laney."

Noah looked taken aback. He darted a quick look around to make sure nobody had overheard before he took Laney's arm to drag her through a doorway out of the banquet room, arriving at the empty elevator lobby.

Laney shrugged his arm off before shooting him an accusing look. "How could you keep something like that from me?" she hissed. "How could you not tell me she died by getting sucked into that freaking swirling vortex of doom?"

Noah's jaw clenched as he furtively looked around again to make sure nobody could hear. "Because some of those details are classified, Laney."

She shot him a flat look. "Seriously? You're going to pull security classification crap with me too?" She shook her head. "I would have thought all that goes out the window when you knowingly endanger someone else's life. And if there was a risk that the quantum shear could possibly kill people, don't you think that—oh, I don't know." She threw up her hands. "You should have told me that *before* you forced me into going into one with you?"

"It didn't happen like that, okay?" he told her, his tone clipped. "The quantum shear is perfectly safe by itself when it's stable," he explained. "And I didn't tell you because...I couldn't risk you not coming back to this world. It was too important."

She stuck her chin up at him. "So tell me now."

Noah sighed a long heavy sigh and replied after a moment. "It was the only way. Can you please keep that in mind? The earlier you already realized that."

"The only way...for what?" She sighed herself, her patience wearing thin.

Noah cursed softly, frustrated, before he looked up to meet her gaze again. "It was the only way to save you. Okay?"

Laney stopped way short. *What?*

He averted his gaze. He knew he was going to have to tell her everything. Laney was nothing if not stubborn, and having been told the highlights, she would no longer simply let up and patiently wait for her memory to come back to find out.

He took a deep breath. "There wasn't time...to save you both."

She paused. "What? What are you saying? You're saying you—saved *my* life, instead of hers?" She was unable to disguise the complete bewilderment and shock on her face as she looked up at him again. "*Why?*"

Noah swallowed hard as he looked at her.

It was a valid question. She could see in his eyes he knew the answer but she could also sense his hesitation. It was as though he couldn't bring himself to say the incredibly confusing answer out loud.

Laney looked off to one side in deep thought, as she tried to even out her breathing. "You said you've saved my life before, but I would have never imagined that you'd had to sacrifice Eleanor's life for it."

Then her eyes lit up in realization and she blew out a breath. "No wonder you hate me."

Noah's chest constricted. "No..." He shook his head.

She gave him a skeptical look. "No?"

He moved closer, making Laney step back so her back was against the wall.

Laney noticed his expression change as he looked down at her. He was standing so close that she could feel how warm he was, and it was as though without meaning to, he was drawing her in.

"I don't hate you," he told her, his voice almost a low groan. And somehow a shadow of a smirk hovered around the corner of his mouth as he added, "Which frustratingly, is in spite of my best efforts."

Laney's heart began to pound harder as she stared up into his piercing blue eyes, trying to arrest the urge to start heaving. "This feels familiar..." she said, under her breath.

"It is," he replied, gazing down at her intently.

17

⁓⧉⁓

A Reminder

Noah's HUD beeped.

And Laney let out a breath she didn't realize she'd been holding, even as she still didn't move an inch, and her gaze shifted toward his hand briefly, before moving up to meet his gaze again.

Noah blinked slowly, before glancing down at his HUD, but not pulling back. "Berry's got something for us back at the lab," he told her. He looked back down at her again, seeming unwilling to break away.

"Hey guys, I just got a message from—whoops!" Maia immediately did an about-face upon seeing Laney and Noah how they were. "Uhh...I better—I'll tell you later—"

"Maia!" Noah called her back sharply as he stepped back a few feet away from Laney.

Laney swallowed hard as she straightened herself up, her

cheeks flaming red when she briefly met Maia's gaze as she turned back toward them.

"Um," Maia began. "I got a message from Berry. He's sending through his own analysis of the chem panels from GNR. It should help us figure out what's wrong with my machine."

Noah nodded. "Then we'd better get back to the University," he said, his tone neutral.

Laney met his gaze for a moment, before she looked over at Maia again, who was pursing her lips, obviously trying to stifle a giggle.

Great. Just great...

Laney could only stand back and watch as Maia and Berry, transmitting through Berry-AI, huddled in front of several reversible, see-through glass panels, full of scientific formulas in different-colored scrawls, as they worked together to analyze the results from that morning's trial of the memory-doohickey reversal chamber, discussing and arguing points between themselves, sounding more and more frustrated as the evening wore on.

"I can still barely understand what they're saying." She glanced sideways over at Noah, who was only leaned against a shelf a few feet away from her.

When he looked up at her, Laney raised her eyebrows in a prompt. "Why doesn't Berry just make Berry-bot solve the formula? Isn't he a smart android?"

"It can only do what it's been programmed to do," Noah replied. "Most AI's generally don't have the capacity for creative thinking, even learning AI's. They can only work on the data they're provided and even then, they can only extrapolate so far. Not enough to help with this type of scientific analysis work."

"I thought you were a 'scientist' too?" She motioned with air quotes. "Why don't *you* help them out?"

"I'm a theoretical physicist," Noah told her pointedly. "My understanding of biochemistry is basic, rudimentary at best. Each of us has our own expertise."

"Sure, like karate chopping some guy into oblivion," Laney quipped to P.T., again perched on the lab table beside her.

Noah just huffed, crossing his arms over his chest again.

"What? But that doesn't make any sense." Maia's forehead was creased. "I thought it was supposed to be T prime equals v squared..."

Berry-AI was making notations on the opposite side of the formulas on the board. "Wait, what if you put *psi* here, and then we can switch this around...like this?" he mused. "And you round off Planck's constant to minus thirty-six instead of thirty-five."

Maia stepped back from the whiteboard, her pen poised in the air in deep thought.

"Well, that's clearly wrong," Laney spoke up from behind her.

Maia turned around, her eyes wide. "Pardon?"

Noah looked up, surprised, as Laney stepped forward to gesture at a particular formula on one of the boards.

"This is obviously in reference to an outdated Pendleton method," she began authoritatively. "His calculations were off by at least .001 or did you forget the paper Wu published last year?"

Maia blinked at her, stunned in disbelief. "P-pardon…?" she asked again.

Noah narrowed his eyes at Laney for a second, before he straightened up in epiphany, just as his HUD began to beep in response to Laney's CCL status. "It's Eleanor," he announced.

Laney turned to him. "What?" she prompted, looking almost annoyed, before turning to the whiteboard to erase the entire formula emphatically. "What are you even doing here, Noah? I thought you said your mission to Abu Dhabi would take three weeks?"

"What's going on?" Maia shot Noah a look of disbelief.

"It's a 'bleed through'. Laney's phased again," Noah told Maia. "To a version of Eleanor apparently."

Maia's eyes widened somewhat in dread. "Shut up."

P.T. whirred on the table, spinning his wheels.

"And seriously, Maia." Laney cast a glance over at a table and wrinkled her nose. "When was the last time you did cell cultures? These look like they were done by a five-year-old."

And Maia rolled her eyes.

Noah just stifled his chuckle. *Captain Blood was back.*

"Berry," Laney snapped. "Would you please be a dear and redo cell cultures five through eight?"

Berry-AI's eyes lit up. "Right away, Dr. Carter," he piped up.

"How do you even know what we're trying to do here?" Maia asked her, sounding almost offended.

Laney shot her a flat look. "You're obviously trying to reverse an enneagram-blocking process using these DNA markers. Anyone with a basic biology degree can tell you that," she said then she waved at the whiteboard. "Although this is an interesting treatment of Wu's work. It looks like you're trying to adapt this formula for an extra-dimensional DNA sample, which is, of course, where everything starts to break down."

If Maia's jaw could drop any more, it would have reached the South Pole.

Noah was just staring at Laney.

He could tell it wasn't *his* world's Eleanor, but she was the same brilliant, candid, almost ruthless Laney that she always was—almost exactly the woman he had fallen in love with. *Almost.*

Noah stepped into the huddle, and with Eleanor's efficient direction and her almost impossibly-perceptive insights, it only took the four of them three more hours to complete what could have taken at least another two weeks' worth of refining formulas and recalibrations for Maia's machine.

When they finished, Laney skimmed her hands as though dusting off imaginary chalk dust. "There you go. Your fancy-ass machine should work properly now." She nodded, looking satisfied.

Maia looked over at Noah and Berry-AI in turn with a smirk. "Um...thanks...Laney," she said.

Laney tilted her head. "Of course," she replied with a haughty smile. Then she looked around the lab and cringed. "I don't know how you can work in such a small space."

Maia cleared her throat, tamping down her offense, and she gave Berry-AI a pointed look. "Berry, why don't you take Laney outside for a little fresh air," she suggested. "I think it might be a little too stuffy in here for her."

"Right away, Dr. Chambers." Berry-AI nodded as he took Laney's arm to lead her out the door.

Noah was shaking his head.

Maia met his gaze. "Did that just happen?" she asked, still in disbelief.

"Don't overthink it," Noah recommended. "We're still not out of the woods."

"What do we do?" she asked. "We can't put Laney in the machine when she's phased like this."

Noah sighed. "I guess we just have to wait." He motioned her toward the machine. "Just make sure the machine is ready. I'll go keep an eye on Eleanor and make sure she doesn't accidentally freak out anyone else from this dimension."

Maia nodded, grinning. "Good plan."

Berry-AI was just leaving when Noah approached the two of them in the same little courtyard from earlier in the afternoon.

"Dr. Donovan," Berry-AI bid him as he walked past, headed back into the building.

Laney was standing by the bench, looking up at the sky, when Noah walked up to her.

"Hey," he greeted.

"Oh, hey Noah," Laney said with a smile before she swept her hand upward across the night sky. "Look at that. Isn't it absolutely fascinating how different the sky could look in the Southern Hemisphere compared to back at GNR? It really makes you appreciate the circumference of the Earth."

He smiled a little. "Sure."

He *did* miss her. Of course, he did.

He cleared his throat softly before asking, "Do you have any idea what's really going on right now?"

"Listen, I've figured it out," Laney began, before she looked up to meet his gaze. "I'm not really supposed to be here, am I?"

Noah blinked at her keen perception then he just shook his head, chuckling. "You've always been such a giant know-it-all."

That made her laugh then she tilted her head slightly as if in deep thought. "But somehow, I get the feeling that *this* Laney is also not supposed to be here," she guessed.

Noah paused for a moment, his expression clearing before he nodded.

Laney looked a bit staggered, as though she had already managed to extrapolate where her real self might possibly be in that case. "I see." She nodded, her tone somber. She shrugged, cracking a small smile. "Well, I suppose it's good to be back, in some way," she said, going to sit down on the bench.

Noah went to sit beside her. Like always.

After a moment, Laney glanced up at him again with another genuine smile. "Did you think we would ever get here?"

"What do you mean?"

Her smile widened. "I mean, a few years ago, all of this—inter-dimensional travel and phasing—was just an idea," she said, looking back up at the sky. "A little theory we would discuss on and off."

Noah raised his eyebrows. "Discuss?" he echoed. "By that do you mean: you'll say something, I'll disagree, and then you'll tell me why I'm wrong?" he asked, his tone sarcastic but good-humored.

That made her laugh.

His smile faded a bit. "I always knew we would get here," he said. "Because you *were* always right, Laney."

She met his gaze again, her expression ambiguous, and she paused before she spoke again. "I'm guessing given the current circumstances, I've made at *least* one mistake."

Noah just looked at her. He knew he didn't have to say anything. Laney was the one person who knew him better than anyone else in the world.

She averted her gaze again. "Do you miss her?"

He replied right away. "Of course I miss you."

Laney pursed her lips, smiling as though she could see right through him. "I think she's coming back now," she said, her voice soft.

Noah's eyebrows furrowed. "Laney, I..." He hesitated. "I really do miss you."

And Laney gave him a haunting smile back. "Don't worry," she said. "The Laney you love will always be with you."

Noah's HUD beeped again.

* * *

Laney blinked slowly, before straightening up in her seat, looking confused as she looked up sideways, upon realizing that Noah's arm was around her shoulders. "Noah? What's—?"

He withdrew his arm. "You phased again."

"Oh."

"To Eleanor."

"Oh." Laney's eyes widened.

"And—she fixed Maia's machine," Noah said with a slight shake of his head, a small, proud smile on his mouth.

"Oh." At that, Laney's stomach tightened. "But of course she did." She took a deep breath. "Maia did say that she was probably the one person who could fix everything," she recalled.

But for some reason, she also remembered something the President had said earlier that night.

Not if you're going to make me feel like I'll be in his shadow forever...

Laney frowned but then she quickly shook her head to clear it. "So?" She sat up straighter. "No point sitting around here then. If Eleanor's fixed the machine, let's get this show on the road."

"Don't people sleep in this world?" Laney was shaking her head, glancing back at all the night owls of the University.

There were still about a dozen people in the common area, studying, working, or having a late-night coffee. A handful of people were still bustling around the hallways despite the late hour.

Maia looked up from her microscope at the sound of Laney's voice, as she and Noah walked into the lab.

"Maia," Noah called. "Laney's back."

"Sssooo..." Laney prompted Maia as she walked up to her with a tickled grin. "I heard *Eleanor* made a 'bleed through' and helped you fix your machine."

Maia shrugged, her face sullen. "Yes, and she was the same goddamn bitch I remember."

That made Laney laugh.

Maia stood up from her seat at the table, walked up to

the memory-doohickey reversal chamber then tilted her head slightly to gesture Laney over. "Are you ready?"

Laney looked bemused. "Does it matter?"

Maia just chuckled as Berry-AI walked up to assist in configuring the panels, with P.T. just looking on.

Laney felt Noah's hand on her back as he came up from behind to help her get into the machine again. She looked up at him, but he didn't say anything. He didn't have to.

The tension in his eyes was more than there was in the morning during the first time around. And she knew just how badly they both wanted this session to succeed.

Laney stepped into the machine, then looked over to meet Maia's gaze too.

The expression on her face was as plain as anyone's. She knew if the machine still didn't work, they were all at a dead end, and Laney would be screwed.

"Alrighty. Here goes nothing," Maia said, pausing for effect before she pushed the button.

****

"Are you okay?" Maia called loudly from outside the chamber once the session had completed.

The door slid open with a hiss and Laney blinked a few times, trying to get her bearings.

Noah stepped up to the door to help her out. "Do you remember anything?" he asked. "How do you feel?"

Laney glanced up at Noah hesitantly. "Um, fine, I guess..."

Maia did her basic checks, her forehead creasing. "I think

we should give her some time to decompress," she suggested. "It looks like the second round took a heavier toll on her."

P.T. chirped from its perch on the lab table.

Berry-AI came over to take Laney's arm. "Perhaps Miss Carter would like to take a little walk," he said, leading her promptly toward the door.

And Noah met Maia's gaze again in an expectant prompt, but she just shrugged. "I know as much as you. I'm afraid all we can do again, for now, is wait."

Noah went to the door to watch as Berry-AI took Laney on a slow walk around the common area, then she must have said something to dismiss him as Berry-AI began to step away, turning to head back to the lab.

Laney's head felt like it was split in two. She didn't need a walk. She *should* have asked for a painkiller.

She happened to glance back at the doorway to Dr. Chambers' lab to see Noah and Maia watching her from across the way, with worried looks on their faces.

For a brief paranoid moment, Laney formed an instant aversion toward them, as she imagined they were probably more likely to be worried about the procedure having worked than they were worried about her actual well-being.

She braced her hand upon a railing, feeling nauseous, and a powerful wave of homesickness hit her again. She missed her family. She missed her friends—the *real* Darla and Kevin, whom she 100% knew would have had her back no matter what.

Meanwhile, everyone in this world seemed preoccupied with keeping secrets and only looking out for themselves.

Laney felt herself starting to heave.

She looked around as her surroundings began to overwhelm her senses.

She felt as though the entire world was spinning around her, she could barely stand upright, and her heart began to hammer in her chest in a flashback of dread, panic, fear, and then somehow...resolution.

She remembered.

She remembered *everything*.

She blinked, disoriented, almost hyperventilating. Then from across the way, her panning gaze screeched to a stop at the same time that Noah glanced up and met her gaze.

Noah registered the look of shock and recognition on her face instantly. His forehead creased as he swallowed hard.

Laney's breathing started to even out as he held her gaze, and after a moment, she felt a small smile on her face.

Noah broke off from talking to Maia and hurried across the lobby toward Laney, but he stopped about three feet away from her. "Hi."

Laney bit her smile back. "Hi."

"Everything...okay?" he wanted to know, narrowing his eyes at her as though to try to determine if she was okay with remembering everything that had happened, everything that had happened between them, and everything since.

She nodded, taking a very deep breath. Then she started to shake her head in disbelief and gave him a wry look. "So much for going back to my normal life, huh?" she started. "I guess that particular great idea didn't quite work out."

Noah couldn't bite back his smile of relief. He almost took a step closer but stopped short, and instead stuck his hands in his pockets. "Listen, I wanted to say I'm—sorry again, about the kiss...the other day..." He looked uncomfortable.

Laney's stomach instantly fluttered at the mention of it.

But Noah went on. "That was just—" He tried to dismiss with a wave. "I was glad to see you. And I..." He hesitated. "I missed...Laney."

Laney frowned a little. *He meant Eleanor.* "Right. Of course." She nodded again.

Then she grimaced. "I'm sorry I didn't remember you right away. I—can't believe how stupid I've been sounding these last few days. And by that," she added. "I mean even *more* stupid than I usually must sound to you guys."

He shook his head. "You didn't. It wasn't your fault."

"But I thought it was all over. I was never supposed to see you again," Laney said, a bit of irritation creeping into her tone, and it was as though the second shoe had dropped as she took full stock of her present circumstances.

She was back. She was stuck. And someone was trying to kill her.

Again.

Laney blew out a breath, happening to glance up across the lobby toward Maia and Berry-AI, waiting by the lab door-way. She sighed. "I suppose we'd better tell them the good news," she said.

It was Berry, transmitting through Berry-AI, who greeted Laney as she and Noah walked back into Maia's lab. "So glad to finally have you back, Laney!" he said with a big smile.

Laney pursed her lips, giving him a tired look. "No offense, Berry, but I'm really not glad to be back."

"How's the recall?" Maia's eyebrows were raised. "Would you say you remember everything completely? Or are some things still hazy in your mind?"

Laney looked at each of them in turn, looked around at the lab, still taking everything in.

She felt like she had been a completely different person for the last eight months and she didn't even know it. "I think it's mostly back," she said, stopping short to groan. "I'm feeling a bit...weak," she said, making a face.

"Flushing out those enneagram blockers will do that to you," Berry-AI said, trying to sound consoling, his nose wrinkled.

"Yep, you definitely should lie down," Maia instructed, coming up to take her arm.

"Don't tell me, you have a futon in your lab."

"Of course I do." She grinned. "But I'm taking you to the on-call room. It's where transient scientists and lecturers stay during their visits to the University. I mean, I'd offer you my futon," she relayed. "But I still need to work on your chem panels to make sure I didn't damage you any further, and you're going to need someplace quiet to rest."

As Maia led her to step out of the lab, Laney glanced back at Noah and Berry-AI.

Berry-AI was giving him a sympathetic look. "Give her a moment," he advised. "Can't even imagine the shock to her system having just recovered those particular memories."

And before Laney was out of earshot, she caught their last exchange.

"She's going to be different again."

"She'll still be Laney."

Laney's pulse seemed to race intermittently, even as she was just lying down on the bed in the otherwise empty on-call room.

She figured her frazzled nerves must have to do with gaining back memories of the last time she was here, as though with each piece of memory, an associated emotion also needed to be reintegrated back into her. It felt exhausting, but it was definitely keeping her awake.

Laney stopped short as she caught sight of Noah out the door, across the hallway.

It looked like he'd just had a shower.

He had taken off his usual heavy flight jacket, having changed into a cotton T-shirt that, whether he meant for it to or not, showed off his muscular, but lean figure.

She felt her heart pound from the vivid, recently recovered memory of what being pressed against his chest had felt like. Especially as she also realized what the dream about 'sparks' had all been about.

Her face flushed hot upon realizing she now possessed two distinct memories of having been kissed by him.

For god's sake, get a grip, she scolded herself again.

P.T. whirred softly in its "nest", half-buried under Laney's trench coat, which was in a heap on an empty bed.

Laney shot it a sharp look. "Shut up, P.T."

She looked away, rolling over in bed, sighing, as she

thought about Kevin—the Kevin from her world, her actual boyfriend, whom she may in fact, never see again.

The last eight months with him had been really good. She wondered if they still would have been had she retained all of her memories from the last time she was here.

She shook her head quickly to clear it. *Jeez, where's that forgetting serum when you need it?* Couldn't they have just selectively brought back her memories of her time here—that was, without any of the ones with Noah in them?

She wanted to think that her anxiety was caused by it all just being too confusing because of course, it was.

But what she was really more afraid of was that perhaps the reason for her anxiety was because she actually wasn't confused at all. About anything. Not even a little bit.

Noah was beyond exhausted.

All he wanted to do was pass out on one of the remaining beds in the sparsely-furnished on-call room, with only two chairs and the two bunk beds in it, and Laney fast asleep in one of the bottom bunks. But instead, he looked out the window, in deep thought.

It was still dark outside, but it was almost dawn again.

They had succeeded in getting Laney her memories back. The mission was half-done. And he knew in the morning, they would have to plan out the next steps of fixing Laney's displacement.

So she could go home, back to her own world. Permanently.

He felt frozen, paralyzed in disquiet.

"Noah...?"

Noah turned toward the sound, a bit surprised to hear Laney call his name. He'd thought she was deep asleep.

Laney blinked as she looked up at him, slowly sitting up in bed. "Noah?" she asked again, looking incredulous.

"Yeah." He walked over to the side of her bed to ask if she needed anything.

But before he could speak again, Laney threw her arms around him. "Oh my god, Noah, is that you?"

He looked down at her. "What's going on?"

"Oh my god, you have no idea what I've been going through! I thought you were dead!"

"What? What are you talking about?" he asked, confused, moving to sit down beside her.

"What do you mean?" she implored, looking up at his face. "Blakely's guys attacked us outside The Louvre," she said, her voice breaking. "Those drones chased us, then their airship came and—and..." She grimaced. "You got shot. I thought...I thought you died. I saw you die..."

Noah's mouth dropped open slightly as he recalled that memory exactly, but what he remembered was that Laney had pushed him away just as one of the trackers had shot at him. Laney had saved him that day too.

He paused, his hands braced on her shoulders as he looked down at her face.

Laney had "phased" again, and somehow, this was a Laney from another alternate version of this world, one where Noah had in fact, not survived the Paris encounter.

"I saw it," she said, tears starting to roll down her cheeks. "It was so horrible!" She buried her face in his chest. "I didn't know what to do. I was so scared!"

Noah swallowed, but he didn't move.

It struck him how incredibly lucky they had actually been in Paris—in *this* dimension—as it easily could have been much, much worse.

He realized that there could also have been a world wherein *this* Laney would have died in Paris instead.

His stomach tightened as he was again struck by the thought of there being a very real possibility of losing her. And it could all happen so easily. The mere notion of it made him feel nauseous.

Then Laney quieted. She pulled away and looked up at him again, her eyes adjusting to the dim light. "Noah? What...are you doing here?" She wiped her face with the back of her hand, surprised to find it wet. "What—why am I crying?"

Noah straightened up in his seat, somewhat in relief. Laney was back again. "You had another 'bleed through'."

"Oh great." She groaned. "What the hell did I do now? Transform into G.I. Jane and try to kill you again?"

"No." He shook his head. "No. You just..." He hesitated. "It was a version of you from a world where I didn't survive the attack in Paris."

She gasped. "Oh my god. That sounds...horrible."

"But I did survive it," Noah relayed. "At least, in *this* world, I did." He tilted his head slightly, looking at her. "Because you saved me."

Laney met his gaze, recognizing the shift in his tone.

Then he said, "It's all my fault."

"What is?"

"Your condition," he supplied. "I'm the reason you're displaced."

He sighed as he began. "You got shot by an energy beam when we entered that first quantum shear. When I had misled you into thinking that I needed your help to save Eleanor and coerced you to come to this world with me. All these 'bleed throughs' are happening to you now because you had pushed me out of the way. I should have been hit by that energy beam. But instead, you were."

He met her gaze again. "You saved my life, right from the start."

He wasn't touching her at all, but he was sitting next to her, leaned in close enough that he was sure she could feel his energy, his warmth, radiating from him, enveloping her.

"That was when I knew...I could never have given you up to Blakely," Noah said softly. "Laney, I knew...it was you," he said, his gaze dropping down to her mouth.

Laney was starting to heave.

About a zillion emotions zinged through Noah. He was totally in love with Eleanor. And he knew Laney totally had a boyfriend. This was totally wrong. But it was completely overwhelming. And she'd always had this effect on him.

Even when she didn't even remember who he was. She didn't even belong to this world. And she definitely didn't belong to him. And yet...

But just as Laney's eyelids fluttered and she moved to touch his face, Noah stopped abruptly, straightening up in his seat, and he shifted back.

Then he blinked a few times, not looking at her. "I'm sorry," he said before he stood up and disappeared out the door.

18

The Fix

Noah hadn't slept a wink.

"Can you make the coffee any stronger than that?" he asked Berry-AI.

Berry-AI didn't need any sleep. But he watched Noah in assessment as he put another spoonful of coffee grounds into the coffee maker.

Noah kept staring at him.

And Berry-AI moved to put yet another spoonful into the paper cup before Noah turned away. Berry-AI watched him strangely for another moment before he pressed the 'Go' button.

It was too early in the morning for all the night owls in the University to be up and about. It was probably the only time of day when the campus was as quiet.

Maybe a little too quiet. As there was nothing going on to distract Noah from the burden of his own thoughts.

He had long been struggling with the guilt that it was entirely his fault that Laney was displaced from her world and stuck there to begin with.

And the worst part was that deep down he knew, he didn't even want her to get cured either. He didn't want her to go back to her world. He wanted her to stay.

He shook his head briskly to clear the thought.

Selfishness was what had gotten everyone to this point to begin with. Eleanor's. His.

Noah had been too selfish to think of Laney's well-being from the get-go, dragging her into his world just to help him to rescue Eleanor from Blakely, regardless of the consequences—even if it turned out that the consequences were in fact, pretty darn apocalyptic.

Nothing he'd ever done had ever turned out well for Laney. He wanted to kick himself. He needed to protect her. He needed to stay away.

Except he knew, between the two of them, it was already proving to be an uphill battle.

Maia had been dozing in her futon in the corner of the lab for a couple of hours since having completed some analysis on the results of Laney's second session in the memory-doohickey reversal chamber in the early hours of the morning.

"Good morning, Dr. Chambers," Berry-AI called out as soon as he spotted Maia stirring and getting up from her futon.

But Maia walked straight up to a console to set it up to analyze the next and last set of chem panels. "Last one," she mumbled, even as she waved her hand behind her, not looking up to call out. "Can I have some coffee too please?"

"I sent Dr. Vermillion the readouts from earlier this morning, Dr. Chambers," Berry-AI relayed as he poured her a cup of coffee. "He should be in touch to discuss the results later today."

Maia walked up toward the lab table that had been converted into a breakfast counter, before she glanced over at Noah, sitting on a stool at the end, his dour mood only then registering with her. "What's up with you?" she wanted to know.

Noah looked away. "Nothing," he said, brooding over his cup of coffee.

Maia watched him for a moment. "Fine," she said. "In case, you were interested to know, according to the latest chem panels, Laney seems to be in ship shape. Hopefully, in ship-shapier shape than before."

"Great."

Maia just rolled her eyes in resignation. She turned to Berry-AI. "I found an interesting pattern in Laney's brain wave activity. Do you know if Berry can help do some extrapolations back at GNR?"

"*I'll* send the message, Dr. Chambers," Berry-AI replied. "Perhaps you could also reach out to Dr. Whitfield. *My* search indicates he is the closest local expert on modeling projections."

Maia considered it with a nod. "Thanks, Berry-bot." She reached for a bagel on a plate, with the bagel going straight to her mouth for a big bite. "Hey, isn't Laney awake yet?" she asked, her voice muffled by the bagel, as she craned her neck to look around. "We talked about having waffles today."

Noah stiffened, feeling a sudden wake-up jolt in his system, better than the coffee, already somehow in dread. He quickly flicked up his HUD to get a GPS location on Laney's CCL, and his eyes widened in alarm as an instant panic seized him.

"What is it?" Berry-AI peered at the HUD sideways from across the table.

"I'm not getting any reading on her CCL," Noah said, his tone grim before he looked up to meet Maia's gaze.

But Maia's eyes were wide as she stared at the HUD on Noah's arm. "What...the hell is that?" she asked, looking taken aback. "Why do you have one of those?"

Noah froze. He had momentarily forgotten that he wasn't meant to show his HUD around The Community.

But Berry-AI's eyes were moving rapidly from side to side. "*I* am also unable to track Miss Carter's location," he stated.

"Laney's locator must have been turned off altogether," Noah concluded, swallowing hard.

There was only one group of people he knew of who would know enough not to just jam Laney's CCL signal, but disable it entirely.

Maia put her hand up. "Hold on a minute," she interjected. "What the heck is going on? Laney is gone? Where did she go? And why *on Earth* do you have one of those?"

Noah gave her an even look. "Do you know what this is?"

Maia bit her lip, seeming unwilling to reply.

Noah stood up fast. "We're wasting time," he said, reaching for his jacket draped over the back of a chair. "Laney's life is in danger."

"What?" Maia asked, frowning. "Why? Where is she?"

"I don't know where she's been taken, but I definitely know by whom," Noah replied as he hastily stuffed his pockets with certain gadgets. "Come on, Berry-bot." He waved him over. "If they got to her this fast, the odds are The Alliance has a headquarters right here in town."

Maia shot him a mocking look as she stood up herself, turning around to watch them. "That's a myth! They don't exist."

Noah just gave her a steady look, even with the urgency in his tone. "Maia, you just stay here in case Laney comes back," he ordered.

"Seriously?" she called out after them as they rushed out, but they were gone in seconds. Maia threw up her hands in exasperation, looking around the empty lab. "What just happened?"

***

Laney moaned softly as she woke up, but even with her eyes still shut, she could already tell exactly what the smell was that was overpowering her senses.

The smell of old books.

"What...?" She opened her eyes, confused, only to find that she was waking up sitting upon a steel chair, with her wrists and ankles clamped to it with metal restraints. "What?" She tried to shake off the restraints to no avail. Her pulse began to race in dread as she looked around.

The building where she was at was obviously a library— or what would have previously served as a library, if not for all the mostly empty bookshelves, the sagging platforms up on the third and fourth floor, the tall columns propped up with temporary supporting steel girders, all the boarded-up windows and doorways—and of course, the dozens of Alliance agents hanging about, standing guard.

Laney spotted the one called Jacob across the open-plan reading room on the ground floor, talking to a female Alliance agent with long red hair.

"Are you sure we have the right, Laney?" Jacob was asking her.

"Positive," she replied. "You can't fool Noah. He definitely fetched the right one." Then she looked over at Laney to notice that she was awake. "Jacob," she said.

And Jacob turned around. He smiled when he met her gaze, spreading out his arms as though to gesture around him. "Miss Carter," he began. "How lucky you must feel to finally be around people who are true to their word."

Laney glared at him in disbelief. "Sure, that's the word I'm looking for right now. Lucky," she remarked.

He walked up toward her, observing her attempts to pull free from her restraints. "So sorry about that, by the way," he remarked. "What with all your 'bleed through' personas, we couldn't take any chances."

"*Sorry?*" Laney echoed indignantly. "You kidnapped me!" she exclaimed.

"Nuh-uh." Jacob shook his head. "As a matter of fact, you came here on your own," he told her. "Of course, it took a little bit of creative hacking on our end."

Laney's eyes widened. "You *hacked* my CCL!" she realized. "Oh my god, people have got to stop playing around with my brain! And how in the freaking world," she cried out, still trying to rattle her restraints off, "do you all have this type of chair?"

That made Jacob chuckle. He glanced up at the red-headed girl again. "She's funny," he noted. "Laneys aren't usually funny."

The red-headed girl smirked before she glanced back down at the control panel she was working on. "We need your confirmation on the go-ahead order," she told him, and he nodded in acknowledgment.

Laney squinted to see. It looked like Jacob was tapping on invisible keys in mid-air upon a HUD of his own on his left arm. She grimaced. "What is that? Is that a...HUD?" she asked, looking baffled. "I thought Noah had the only one. It was supposed to be a prototype."

Jacob glanced up at her. "Is that what he told you?" he asked, sounding highly entertained. "Oh boy, that Donovan is such a master of deception."

"What the hell are you talking about?" Laney prompted, already annoyed at his ambiguity. "Did you steal that HUD from him?"

"Oh, sweetie." Jacob gave her a look. "Where do you think Noah got his?" he quipped. "Only Alliance carry this tech."

Laney's stomach turned over and her pulse began to race again in disbelief. "What the hell are you saying? That Noah is in The Alliance?"

"Jacob," the red-headed girl called out. "We're ready."

Laney's eyes lit up as she looked over at her. "What does that mean? Ready for what?"

Jacob beamed at her. "The fix, of course."

A couple of agents walked over to secure Laney, as her restraints unclipped with a loud click, and they pulled her up, taking her arms on each side.

"The fix of what?" Laney asked, her eyes still wide in dread, even as she let the two agents escort her across the reading room to a corner where the old sign for 'Photocopying' was still hanging, except for instead of a photocopying machine, what was there was a strange-looking metal bed with a curved bottom.

"I understand you're not very happy in this dimension, Miss Carter," Jacob said as he walked over to the machine with her. "And no doubt you've sensed that despite how pretty it looks on the surface, this world is a mask—a fact that even the people living in it don't want to acknowledge themselves. Fortunately for you," he said with a smile. "This isn't your world. And we're simply trying to facilitate your departure from it as expediently as possible."

Laney remembered how Noah said their expedience might possibly affect her—as in *permanently* and she began to try to struggle away from their grasp.

"No, no, no." She shook her head, starting to panic. "Please don't. Please, oh my god, this can't be happening to me again," she said, as horrible flashbacks of the giant quantum jump platform receptacle back at GNR raced through her mind.

But a third agent came up to help hold Laney up as they half-dragged her toward the metal bed and carried her in, quickly fastening her feet onto the bed.

Laney glanced up to give Jacob an imploring look. "But I'm not contagious yet," she told him. "Berry will come up with a cure soon. Please. Please! The 'bleed throughs' have only just started," she tried to reason, even as another agent pushed her to lie down so they could fasten her wrists.

Jacob rolled his eyes. "Please, you've been displaced right

from the beginning," he told her. "Try to think back. The 'bleed throughs' have been happening even since the last time you were here. You've been an anomaly for eight months. Why do you think Blakely's quantum jump platform wouldn't work with you? You were already displaced at the time."

She swallowed hard as she absorbed his words. *What?* She wanted to speak up to protest again, except the memory of Paris flashed vividly in her brain, and she blinked in recognition. No wonder everything had felt so familiar.

Jacob was right.

Shit. Laney heaved in anxiety, even as she tried to pull against the clamps on her hands and feet in vain.

"Now just relax," he advised. "The biobed will cure all your ills." He reached over to shift down a curved metal arc to prop around Laney's head.

Laney felt incredibly helpless, and tears were starting to roll down her cheeks.

Just then, Laney heard a familiar beep, and she stopped short. *What the hell?*

"What was that?" the red-headed girl asked, looking up from her control panel.

Jacob was looking around furtively. "What is that? Is that the smoke detector?" he asked. "Oi, Teina!" He waved his hand at one of the other agents. "Go to the back and check the fuse box."

Whatever it was beeped again.

"It's coming from this room, Jacob," the red-headed girl told him as she had paused, her head tilted slightly, straining to hear.

Jacob began to walk around the room, trying to zone in on

the strange beeping sound. He lingered near the boarded-up revolving front doors leading to the outside and narrowed his eyes. "What is that...?"

Laney was trying to peer up from the bed to see what Jacob was doing.

The thing beeped again.

Jacob sauntered across the room, toward where Laney's jacket was heaped haphazardly onto a chair in the corner, before brusquely tossing it aside to uncover a little metal robot with exposed gears and spokes.

P.T. had been hiding in Laney's coat pocket the entire time.

P.T.! Laney almost screamed in absolute relief.

"It's a little robot!" the red-headed girl exclaimed in dismay, and she noted the blinking red light on its 'head'. "And it's got a locator beacon, Jacob. It's been spying on us the whole time. Noah will have tracked this robot. He'll know exactly where we are!"

"You sneaky little—" Jacob snatched P.T. off the chair in anger, before immediately hurling it across the room.

"NO!" Laney cried out, aghast.

But it was too late.

The little robot hit the wall squarely, smashing against it, sending pieces of metal and fragments flying around, falling to the floor in unrecognizable heaps. A few bits and pieces whirred softly for a few seconds before each gear and mechanism stopped dead completely.

Laney heaved heavily, her chest constricting, a lump in her throat. She turned to glare up a Jacob. "You big jerk!"

"That's enough," Jacob growled. "We're out of time." He

walked up to the control panel himself, pushed a button, and the biobed began to emit a loud, steady hum.

"No! No!" Laney tried to struggle against her restraints but it was no use.

Out of the corner of her eye, she could see a bright yellow glow form at her feet and start to slowly move its way up her body. It almost looked like the golden halo glow from Maia's memory-doohickey reversal chamber, except for—

"Aaahh—aagghh!" Laney started to seize in the machine as excruciating pain began to explode from within her.

The red-headed girl looked over at Jacob warily. "What's going on, Jacob?"

Jacob looked stunned. "I don't know."

The red-headed girl's palm hovered over the 'Off' button. "Should we stop it?"

"No," Jacob yelled out. "Just let it finish."

Laney kept screaming in pain as the yellow glow had come halfway up her body.

"Her vitals are going ballistic," the red-headed girl spoke up, sounding alarmed, as several control panels began to give off shrill warning beeps. The machine was being overloaded. "Jacob!" she yelled out. "What do we do? Jacob!"

All the sounds began to mute to Laney, and she felt as though she was starting to float out of her body, even as the constant unbearable pain was coursing through her, she didn't have enough strength left to scream.

There was a sudden loud crash and when Jacob looked up, he spotted Noah rappelling down through the broken skylight, just as Noah shot an energy beam from a weapon directed straight at the control panel where the red-headed girl was standing.

The panel exploded and the girl yelped aloud, falling back on the floor.

The biobed shut off instantly.

A couple of agents tried to rush toward Noah, but not before Berry-AI rappelled down next, landing flat on all of them.

Noah glanced up at him. "Thanks, dude."

Berry-AI grinned. "*No problemo, amigo.*"

Noah hurried straight toward the biobed where Laney was unconscious.

Except, Jacob knew that was exactly what he was going to do, so he had aimed his weapon toward him and fired.

Berry-AI leaped across to block the energy beam and he fell back as the shot hit him squarely in the chest. "Agh—!" was the only sound he managed to make before he crumpled to the ground.

"Berry!" Noah yelled as about a dozen agents began to descend on him. He moved quickly, climbing onto an empty bookshelf before he fished something from his pocket, tossing it down to the floor.

POOF!

And all the Alliance agents collapsed, out cold, on the tiled library floor.

Noah glanced up, spotting movement up on the second floor.

Jacob was upstairs with the red-headed girl, getting ready to run away out the fire exit. He met Noah's gaze. "You know we'll be back for her again," he called out. "We are duty-bound not to stop until she's removed from this world. One way or another," he vowed. "She's a threat and you know it."

Noah sneered at him. "Thanks for the warning."

He didn't bother to watch them escape. He jumped down and skidded to a stop beside the biobed to check on Laney, leaning over her.

With the machine off, her restraints had unclamped themselves. But he couldn't check her vitals effectively since his own heart was pounding in his chest.

He was still heaving. "Laney." He shook her shoulders, but she didn't respond.

She didn't seem to be breathing.

Laney looked dead.

"No, Laney no," he urged. "Come back. Come back to me." He shook her shoulders harder. "Come on!" He swallowed hard, looking around, feeling extraordinarily, unusually helpless.

He knew he only had a few minutes before The Alliance agents woke up again from their enforced nap.

He leaned over her face. "Laney, come on," he whispered, still breathless, pressing his forehead against hers, squeezing his eyes shut. "Please...if you die too, I don't know what I'm going to do."

Only the silence of the library answered him.

After another moment, Noah took a deep resigned breath, trying to dull the acute pain in his chest as he began to think of a plan of how to carry both Laney and the broken Berry-AI out of the library.

His head shot up when he heard a small moan—coming from Laney. "Laney?" he prompted again, a lump in his throat.

Laney's chest rose and fell and she made another faint moaning sound.

And Noah blew a breath out in relief, blinking hard.

Laney was alive.

19

Theoretically

Berry-AI looked a bit silly with a giant battery cell plug sticking out of his side as he walked up to Noah who was brooding in the hallway of the infirmary wing of the University. He tilted his head to peer at what Noah was discreetly looking at on his HUD.

Pictures of Noah and Eleanor.

"What are you doing?" Berry-AI prompted, his tone mocking. "Are you still pining over Eleanor? Laney is *alive*."

Noah jumped upon hearing his voice, putting away his HUD quickly. He looked up, narrowing his eyes at Berry-AI. "Berry, is that you?"

Berry-AI rolled his eyes. "Of course it's me," he replied. "Now why aren't you in there?" he asked, gesturing toward the room where Laney had been recovering for the last eighteen hours.

Noah looked up through the window in time to see Laney

laugh at something that Maia said, while Kevin stood by her side, arranging a bouquet of flowers by her bed. His forehead creased. "I'm confused enough as it is, okay?"

"How long are you going to pretend she's not the one you want?" Berry-AI threw up his hands.

Noah shot him a pointed look. "You said it yourself. The effects of the cure will be irreversible," he reminded him. "Once she gets rooted back to her world, I'll never see her again. But if she stays here, The Alliance is going to kill her," he concluded in frustration. "Either way, I'm going to lose her. And I don't want to lose her too."

"So, what—you're just going to sulk here on the sidelines forever? Super lame, man," Berry-AI remarked, shaking his head. "You need to tell her. Tell her what you are."

"No," Noah snapped. "She's free to choose. We both are."

Berry-AI was still shaking his head. "You've both already chosen. You just don't want to admit it."

Noah clenched his jaw and waved him away. "Don't you have some work to do?"

"Actually, I just got the discharge forms." Berry-AI held up the piece of paper. "I'm about to tell them. Don't you want to come in?"

Noah simply grunted his reply and moved to walk away in the opposite direction.

"Suit yourself." Berry-AI shrugged as he turned to head into Laney's room.

"Berry!" Laney cheered when he entered.

"Hi guys," Berry-AI greeted with a smile. "Good news! Laney can go home now."

Laney's eyes lit up instantly. "What?"

"What?" Maia and Kevin's eyes were wide too.

Berry-AI was flustered. "Oh, oops, I mean," he said, holding up the piece of paper. "She's being discharged."

"Oh." Laney's face fell.

Berry-AI made a sheepish face, smacking his forehead with his palm. "I'm so sorry. I can be such a doof sometimes."

Laney chuckled, shaking her head. "Don't worry about it," she dismissed. "Anyway," she said. "I told you guys I was feeling much better." Then she looked up at Berry-AI again, frowning. "I'm just still sad about P.T."

Berry-AI put his hand on Laney's shoulder. "Don't worry about P.T.," he assured. "We can rebuild him. We have the technology."

Laney turned to him with an amused look. "Is that a 'Six Million Dollar Man' reference?"

Berry-AI's expression was blank. "Six million what?"

And Maia and Kevin exchanged puzzled looks.

Laney bit back her mirth as Kevin assisted her off the bed. "Never mind."

"Hey, I thought Berry-bot short-circuited when he got shot too?" Maia wanted to know.

"Its power cell just overloaded," Berry explained through Berry-AI. "So it'll have to be deactivated as soon as we get it back to your lab. I'll need to construct a new regenerative power cell for it. In fact, this temporary battery is dying out already so I'll have to sign off now."

"Okay, Berry," Maia bade.

"Tell Noah I'll call again on Maia's lab's holo-phone to discuss next steps," Berry-AI said to them, before he blinked his eyes closed, even as he kept walking with them, headed out the room and down the hall, going back to the main University wing.

Laney was watching Berry-AI walk with his eyes closed. "That is so bizarre," she remarked.

"Even more bizarre than what you've just gone through?" Maia prompted, her eyebrows raised.

Given the circumstances, but only to a certain degree, Maia and Kevin had been let in on what had happened and who had been responsible for Laney's abduction.

"If you hadn't told me yourself, I wouldn't have believed it," Maia said.

"The question is: are you sure you're safe now?" Kevin asked, looking concerned.

Laney was still anxious. "Probably..." She happened to glance up to spot Noah as they walked past the south side of the building.

He was standing by the little courtyard behind the University all by himself.

"Hey guys," she began. "Why don't you go ahead first? I'll just go deliver Berry's message."

Maia made a face. "Noah doesn't look too happy, does he?"

Laney huffed. "I'm starting to get used to it. He scares everyone."

"He doesn't scare me." Kevin met her gaze to give her a reassuring smile.

Laney bit back her smile, even as her stomach fluttered at his response.

Maia smirked. "You know what? Kev and I are going to go get you some waffles," she said. "You deserve a treat for finally being out of the hospital."

Laney laughed. "That sounds great. Thanks."

"See you later, Laney." Maia waved her away with a grin. "This way Berry-bot." She gestured for Berry-AI to follow them into the building.

And Laney shook her head in mirth before she turned around to walk toward the courtyard where Noah was.

Noah was looking up at the statue, as though in deep thought himself.

Laney followed his gaze, an inkling of a memory coming back to her. She pursed her lips. "I do know this place, don't I?" she prompted from behind him.

Noah didn't seem surprised that she was there. He simply nodded. "This is where I proposed to Eleanor last year," he relayed.

She took a deep breath and nodded. "I think...I was there."

He shot her a look, taken aback. "What?"

"I had a dream about this place last year," she explained. "And you. And...*that*," she noted, referring to the proposal. "I think I must have been seeing through Eleanor at the time, in my dreams." She nodded again. "I was there."

Noah's mouth had dropped open.

"Hey," Laney piped up, changing the subject. "Berry said he was going to call you on Maia's lab's holo-phone to discuss next steps—whatever that means." She shrugged. "So we'd better get going." She motioned for them to go back inside.

Noah stared at her for a moment, before he snapped to alert and moved to follow Laney into the building.

"Alright, Mister Wizard," Laney prompted Berry's big talking head on Maia's lab's holographic videophone. "Now that I have my memory back, what next?"

Berry raised his eyebrows. "Now we find your yellow brick road," he replied.

Laney grinned. "I can't believe you understood that reference."

"Please, that was a *pre*-cascade bomb movie—another classic," Berry dismissed.

She chuckled, glancing back over at Noah who had resumed his regular programming, having donned a stoic expression on his face, and looking down to tinker on his HUD.

Laney's smile faded a bit in recall of the information that Jacob had relayed with regards to the HUD, and which sorts of people actually carry them.

She fidgeted slightly, her stomach churning in apprehension, but she ignored the thought for the moment. She averted her gaze to look around the empty lab.

Maia and Kevin were still out and the rest of Maia's lab staff had been sent on lunch break so that Berry could discuss the next steps with Noah and Laney without worrying about anyone overhearing.

Berry had noted Noah's expressive silence again as, as per usual, an indication to move on.

"Uh, right." He straightened up. He looked down to read something from his console. "Well, the good news is, if I'm reading this right, The Alliance was actually onto something.

They'd also figured out, just as I had, that the cause of The Bleed was the initial tracking solution that Eleanor had dosed you with."

"Oy, it's like the gift that keeps on giving." Laney sighed, exasperated.

Berry grinned. "Basically, traces of the tracking solution that Eleanor had used on you when she was running those experiments last year are attracting all your other selves like a homing beacon," he explained. "So we have to flush it all out of you."

"Great!" Laney remarked. "So we just need to extract all the traces of this tracking solution thingy from me and we're home free?" she asked, already looking relieved.

"Um, it's not quite that simple," Berry said, wrinkling his nose.

Laney's face fell. "*Of* course not."

"You were right," Berry told her. "Their biobed was an adaptation of Maia's machine. It isolates and modifies targeted proteins too, except in Maia's version, she only flushes out the tagged memory enneagram blockers that we had planted eight months ago, whereas The Alliance's machine is trying to flush out all the exotic particles of Eleanor's original tracking solution."

He went on. "But the problem was their implementation. The Alliance wasn't able to flush all the exotic particles out of you fast enough before your atomic structure depolarized completely. That's why it hurt so much and you almost..." He cleared his throat instead of finishing his sentence.

Noah shifted, looking uncomfortable, but he didn't say anything.

"So their approach is too slow," Laney concluded.

Berry nodded. "What you need is a strong, sudden shock."

"Great," she piped up. "So what do we need to do?"

"Well..." Berry began. "I have a theory."

And Laney rolled her eyes. "Fantastic, another one of those."

"The math is all there," Berry defended, looking confident. "The preliminary models all support my theory. We just...don't have enough dense mass to create what we need artificially under lab conditions. And—the closest source is about six hundred light-years away."

Noah's eyebrows rose. "So you *have* figured out what level of exposure she'll need in order to reverse the effects of the 'bleed through'?"

Laney narrowed her eyes. Everyone was speaking in English, but again, as always, it seemed like nobody was. "Huh?"

"To put it plainly," Berry began to Laney—supposedly plainly. "When you were displaced, you were exposed to high levels of dark energy. And I think what your system needs is a hyper-intense shock exposure from the opposite kind of energy particle. Such as coming from a..." he trailed off hesitantly.

She blinked. "A what?"

Berry still looked hesitant.

"What, Berry?" Noah pressed, his eyes wide with impatience.

"A supernova."

Laney's eyes nearly popped out of her head. "A wh-what?" she sputtered out. "You—want to expose me...to a supernova?"

Berry shrugged. "Just for a second," he put in, as though it made the matter lighter.

She shot him a look of mocking ridicule. "Oh. Okay."

Just then, there was a loud banging noise coming from behind Berry on the holographic video feed.

"What was that?" Laney wanted to know, squinting to study Berry's background on the screen.

It looked like instead of a lab at GNR, he was inside a large indoor chamber, bathed in soft wavy sparkles of blue light.

"Hell's bells, Berry. Are you on the mobile submersible lab right now?" she prompted.

Berry met her gaze with a smile. "You are correct, Miss Carter. As a matter of fact, I'm on my way there. See you all soon."

***

To be continued... in Book 3.

Do you want some EXCLUSIVE **Selfless series** bonus content?

Join **S. Breaker's Epic Readers Facebook community** now!

Read on for a sneak peek at Selfless: Book 3...

Sneak Peek

FREE YOURSELF (SELFLESS: BOOK 3)

Laney Carter needs to go home. Thanks to her genius scientist "alternate self", she's been stuck on a parallel world, her life in constant peril. Except it seems the journey back will be as dangerous as staying.

***

"Okay so, what now? We go find that 'supernova' you were talking about?" She gestured air quotes for the word in mocking.

"Supernova?" Maia repeated, looking surprised. "You didn't tell me about that."

"Oh." Laney blinked. "Remember that universal translator thing I was doing—"

"Right, you could speak to anyone in any foreign language it seemed, even obsolete ones."

"Yeah, we found out that that was just a side effect of my...condition," Laney phrased carefully. "The thing is, your illustrious Dr. Carter had given me something." Her gaze slid over to Noah's cautiously, but for a change, he didn't seem incensed to defend Eleanor's good name.

He just met her gaze without a word.

Laney looked away, a slight furrow in her eyebrows. She couldn't quite pin it down, but lately, she sensed that something had changed with Noah. Only it was even more disconcerting than normal.

Berry went on when she paused. "Call it interdimensional insulation," he enunciated. "An especially formulated dose of exotic particles. Basically, it made Laney a tracking point of origin. She served as a reference point. Like on a map, you can't give directions unless you have somewhere to start. It was brilliant because it's what made discovering all the other quantum worlds possible."

"Brilliant," Laney echoed with a wry tone.

"But *horrible*," Berry amended with an instant frown. "Of course. Very, very horrible."

Maia chuckled.

"Yes. Anyway," Laney dismissed. "If I don't get all this stuff out of me, well, let's just say that's where the story ends. I'm not going home. I'm not staying here. I'm not going to...*be*." She made a face. "And apparently, according to Berry, only a supernova blast can effectively *reset* me."

"In theory."

Laney turned an exasperated look over at Berry. "Thanks for that."

"Um, I don't mean to ask the stupid question but wouldn't exposure to a supernova oh say, kill you?" Maia's expression was comical.

"Not the way we're going to do it," Berry quipped confidently.

Noah was already busy with the map, pointing to one of the billion stars in the galaxy. "Betelgeuse," he said and some data scrolled rapidly down the screen. But after a moment, he frowned. "I'm not reading any indications with this star. It looks stable. Are you sure this is the one you meant?"

"Oh." Berry looked hesitant. "See, well, actually, I didn't tell you the other part."

Laney tilted her head. "Why am I not surprised?" she drawled.

"When I said I'd detected an impending supernova in the galaxy," Berry began. "I never said I'd found it in this dimension."

***

Enjoyed the preview? **Free Yourself** is available at your favorite online bookstore.

Sneak Peek

THE CURSE OF THE ARCADIAN STONE

She was solely created to guard a legendary relic. But when a rogue thief from Earth disrupts her dreary world, her job might not be the only thing she loses.

***

"What are you doing here?" He was giving me an odd look. "Are you lost?"

I pursed my lips. I really would have come off more credible if I were up in my tree.

"This place is dangerous." He waved me away. "You better get out of here."

I blinked. That was a switch. He was worried about *me*.

When I still didn't reply, he shrugged and turned to head in the direction of the Mystic Lake.

"Halt!" I stepped forward, raising my hand. "You mustn't go any further."

He stopped and turned back to look at me. "Halt...?"

I bit my tongue. I often forgot that languages evolved and that I had to adjust my manner of speaking. "I mean," I began again. "You must not go in that direction if you know what's good for you. If you are seeking the village, it is that way." I pointed in the other direction.

He looked up where I was pointing then back at me. "I've

just been to the village and trust me, babe, this direction is good for me."

I shot him a look of ridicule. *Babe?* I was over three thousand years old.

He continued to walk toward the Lake.

"Wait!" I went after him. "Please do not go any further. You must believe me. This is for your own safety." I tried to keep up with his long strides.

"Look babe, my safety is my business." His tone seemed firm, resolute.

"As the Guardian of this realm, it actually is my business," I declared. "And I am not a...*babe*." I made a face as I said it.

He paused and turned to me. "Oh, you're the guardian," he spoke as if in realization before his expression turned flat. "So?" he quipped and kept walking.

My serene smile faded when I saw that he was not about to cooperate. "Very well." I shrugged, finally spotting my tree and I drifted up to perch onto one of the lower branches as I watched him walk past below. "If you keep going, you will die," I called down to him. "No living creature can withstand the magical barrier around the Mystic Lake."

He stopped walking.

"Are you here for the relic?" I queried with a casual tone, leaning against the tree trunk.

"If that relic is a broken piece of glass, then it looks like I am."

He'd started to walk but stopped again when I went on. "No one who has ever tried to obtain the relic has survived these woods," I announced. "Trust me. It will do you no good to try to get it."

That made him look up at me, way up above him, and I felt my words sink in. I always did feel better up in my tree. The Forest was my territory. I smiled regally down at him.

"What's your name?"

I blinked again, surprised. "The last person who asked me that died too," I replied instead of answering. "He tried to reason about how badly he needed the relic. I'm afraid it does no good to explain to me. I can't help you," I relayed. "I can only warn you. Please leave while you can."

He gave me a critical look, studying me from head to toe before his eyes met mine again. "What's your name?" he repeated, his tone gentler.

"Um..." I was about to explain that I didn't really have a name but then reconsidered. "I was called—Magenta."

***

Enjoyed the preview?

The Curse of the Arcadian Stone: Nameless Fay series is out now.

Other Titles by S. Breaker

S. R. BREAKER

Epic Fantasy series

The Secret of the Phoenix
The Curse of the Arcadian Stone: Nameless Fay

Fantasy Romance

Dragons of Arcadia Series
Arranged to the Fae Warrior (prequel)
Curse of the Dragon Heir
Reign of the Dragon Heir

SARA BREAKER

Sweet Romance

Holiday Blues
Change of Mind
Insert Happy Ending
Just an Alternate
Switch on Christmas
Crushing on You

Sneak Peek

CURSE OF THE DRAGON HEIR

A headstrong Fae mage accidentally sets a mysterious evil demon free but he may be the key to unlocking her powers...

***

"Are you mated yet?" His voice was gruff but deeply rich.

Soleia shot him a glare. "That's none of your business."

The three warrior females exchanged looks.

Oh, great, she thought in derision. Now they were probably going to start rumors about her and the demon. Just what she needed right now. "Thank you for your help." She dismissed the females with a wave before hanging up her cloak and turning back to fix her hair.

His scrutiny was unnerving her and also making her stomach do somersaults.

Stupid stomach. What the hell was wrong with her anyway? He was a cursed, dangerous demon that would destroy them all with one swish of his claws if given half the chance.

She cleared her throat, hurrying to finish grooming so she could exit the cramped indoor space, feeling a bit more cramped than before.

"Let me free."

Her eyebrows rose in incredulity at his words. "So you can kill me and everyone I know?"

He visibly swallowed hard. "I won't."

Soleia gave him a dull look. "Right."

His forehead creased in aggravation. "You don't even know who I am! How do you know it's justified to hold me against my will? How do you know you're not in the wrong here?"

"Look, the only wrong thing I did today was take too long at that dumb wraith forest. I should have ridden faster, fought harder. I should have just left some of the smaller wraiths alone. If I could have just put them to sleep, I could've—" She stopped short, blowing out a frustrated breath.

His eyes narrowed. "I thought you handled yourself quite well."

She gave him a deadpan look. "I know exactly what you're doing. You're trying to ply me with compliments so that I'll feel sorry for you or something and maybe release you from Oma's binding spell. But I'm not that dumb, Curse Boy."

He blinked like he didn't expect her to figure that out and he merely huffed in displeasure and looked away.

Soleia smirked. She was quite enjoying having so much power over him. "What kind of a dumb demon gets trapped on a tree anyway? And then to finally get free of the tree, only to get trapped by a necklace! Is this only the second curse that's been put on you? Or have there been more?"

That set him off.

He growled again, grabbing her by the shoulders and pinning her back against the wall.

She almost rolled her eyes at his futile intimidation efforts. Did he forget one word from her would send him doubling over? She met his gaze, undaunted. "You didn't scare me before. You definitely don't now."

He roared, leaning close to her face. He was clearly displeased, infuriated. "Mark my words," he rasped. "This spell *will* break. And when that time comes, I guarantee you, you *will* be scared. And then you will die."

"Right, whatever. But until then, Curse Boy, your life belongs to me." Soleia gave him a shove to push away but he pressed harder.

He was focused on her mouth. "Dathon," he growled. He spoke near her face. His freshly-showered scent was almost hypnotizing, overwhelming. Her chest heaved against his in her struggle to breathe and he must have noted her heart pounding. His incensed gaze seared into her. "My name is Dathon."

***

Enjoyed the preview? **Curse of the Dragon Heir** is also available to purchase at your favorite bookstore.

* 9 7 8 0 4 7 3 5 6 1 7 3 4 *